point

D.E. Athkins

SCHOLASTIC INC.
New York Toronto London Auckland Sydney

ISBN 0-590-45349-1

12 11 10 9 8 7 6 5 4 3 2 1   2 3 4 5 6 7/9

Printed in the U.S.A.   01

First Scholastic printing, October 1992

Surprise . . .

Char lifted her face, felt his lips against hers.

Kiss me, kill me, she thought, half-angry with herself for getting so scared, half-amused at what a turn-on fear could be.

"Mmm," she murmured, deep in her throat.

How long would she have stayed there in the weightless dark, a good witch being bad? And how bad . . .

She'd never know the answer.

Because a sound made her open her eyes. A wrong sound.

For a flash she couldn't focus.

And a flash was all it took.

The flash of moonlight on the blade coming down.

For Kim, Kim, Kim

THE RIPPER

Chapter 1

"If you don't use it, you lose it. Right?" Cyndi Moray laughed. Her blood-red lips drew back to reveal long, perfect, pointed teeth. Darling little fangs.

Lara Stepford didn't notice. Lara never noticed anything unless it was male and breathing on her.

"Right?" repeated Cyndi, turning full face toward Lara. Her smoky black eyes glittered between black tracks of eyeliner, beneath parallel tracks of black-penciled eyebrows. She shook her ice-pale hair over her pale shoulders. Her black dress was cut tight with a long front slit held together by a single glittering button that winked and winked when she moved.

She was a study in black and white.

Lara looked up at last. She'd been lying on her back on Cyndi's snow-white bedspread, contemplating the pink sheen of polish on her nails, the silver sheen of stockings on her legs. "What?" she asked.

"Wake *up*, Lara! Get with the program. I *said*, if you don't use it, you lose it, right?" Cyndi flashed her fangs again.

Lara opened her eyes wide. "Oh, disgusting! How do you get them to stay on like that? Do they come off? Can you kiss with them on?"

"Trust me, I can kiss with these — or without them. And there are other things besides kissing. Don't you ever think of anything else?"

"Yes," said Lara.

"Like what?"

Lara thought for a minute. Then she smiled slyly. "There are *other* things besides kissing," she said.

"Oh, good. Very good, Lara." Cyndi popped open a container and began to dust glittery powder over her hair and shoulders.

Lara kept smiling angelically. With her big brown eyes and pouty lips, and the ridiculous long blonde wig over her own fluffy golden hair, she really did look like an angel.

Maybe that was what made the guys so trusting around Lara, Cyndi speculated. She eyed Lara. "You know, you don't need that wig to look like a princess — whose wig is it, anyway?"

"Rapunzel had long, long hair," explained Lara patiently. "I'm Rapunzel." She giggled. "Only I can't let anyone climb up it, 'cause if anything happens to it, my mom'll kill me."

"Oh, dear. No one can climb up it? Wills will be so disappointed." Then Cyndi pretended to do a double take: "Lara! Your *mother* wears that wig?" She held up her hand as Lara opened her mouth to answer. "No. Don't tell me. . . ."

Cyndi went back to putting the final touches on her vampire look. Dade Walken and William Lawrence Howell would be arriving any minute. They would be escorted to the library to wait. Not that Cyndi's family ran much to books, but they were wonderful for decoration and looked so *right* in the room with leather chairs and a discreet bar. At least that's what the decorator her parents had hired had said. Her parents put a big premium on other people's taste. Living on borrowed class, her father had said, laughing hugely, but not on borrowed money.

Her father, who was inexplicably home tonight, would probably keep the guys trapped in the library, pouring out drinks, and weird fatherly charm. And Wills, who was Lara's current entertainment for, oh, the next ten minutes, would drink his, making that careful, idle, polite, endless conversation that boys with names like William Lawrence Howell were so good at making. Dade, on the other hand, who was all lies and laughter, would say, no, thank you, he was driving. But the truth was, he just liked saying no. He liked being in control. Dade was very big on control.

Cyndi smiled. Dade. What would it take to make him lose control?

Cyndi liked to push people. See what she could make them do.

3

Her smile widened. Like tonight. She had big plans for tonight. The Halloween dance was only a beginning.

The vampire vixen in the reflection, standing next to the fairy princess, smiled back.

"Come on," said the vampire. "It's Halloween. Let's go down to the library and wait for Prince Charming and Prince Charming."

Rapunzel said, "Prince Charming was in *Cinderella*."

"Give it a rest, Rap," said the vampire. "Let's go. Time to play."

"Wow, it's going to be *sooo* scary," said Rapunzel, turning to follow the vampire out of the room. "I love Halloween."

"But do you love Wills?" quipped the vampire.

Rapunzel frowned. "It's not the same thing," she said.

The vampire shook her head. "Come on," she said. "Let's party."

Across Point Harbor on the other side of town, Georgina Butler was getting ready for the same dance. And the same party.

Not that she'd been invited to the party exactly. But she knew about it. And she was going to be there. What was Cyndi going to do about it? Throw her out?

She hated Cyndi. She hated a lot of people. She liked hating people. It gave her energy. Courage. A kind of high.

She liked being high.

Besides, plenty of people were less than crazy about Cyndi. Cyndi had a fast mouth and a *lot* of money, and she liked to push people around.

But you can't push me, trendy Cyndi, thought Georgina.

She pulled on the black stockings, slipped on the high black heels. Webs of black moved around her, brushing against her, making her shiver pleasurably. For that night only, she had painted silver streaks in her short, spiked black hair. More webs, black gossamer, floated, caught on the spikes. On the front of her short black turtleneck dress was a red design, an hourglass that she'd carefully painted on herself. On the middle finger of her right hand she wore a spider ring.

The room in which she was getting ready was tiny, a big box, really. The walls were lined with blowups of famous people. There were a lot of Liz Taylor when she'd been young and really gorgeous.

Georgie thought she looked a little like the young Liz Taylor. Maybe a little more like her every day.

Georgie's father thought she was crazy. "Liz Taylor, good grief," he said. "What happened to stars your own age? Like . . . Madonna? Yeah, Madonna?"

Her father. What a loser. No wonder her mother had given him the good-bye. Too bad her mother hadn't thought to take her two-year-old with her.

But two-year-olds were brats. Probably even me, thought Georgie.

Georgie the Black Widow Spider Woman

shrugged. "I'm gonna have a good time tonight," said Georgie.

The doorbell rang.

She went to greet her date. Her very *special* date. Cyndi was going to have a fit when she saw them at her exclusive little party.

Yes. Georgie was going to have a very good time.

"Happy Halloweeen," she cried, throwing open the front door.

Foy Villanova was headed up the stairs of the big old house at the end of the long, long driveway, behind the thick, towering hedges that were so important in this part of the world — the rich part. He smiled, passing those hedges, thinking a little of Sleeping Beauty, maybe, and also of the joke his father told: Those hedges don't grow on trees.

They didn't. They took a long, long time to grow. Old hedges meant old money. Very rich people kept very large houses at very discreet distances behind those hedges. And with that kind of money, anything was possible.

Like him and Jane Wales. Except between them, the possibilities had kind of worn out. He and Jane had known each other all their lives. They'd done a little obligatory fumbling. But basically they'd come up just friends.

Just friends.

Why did people say just friends? Friends lasted. The trouble was, he and Jane might not be able to last. Might not be able to be just friends. She might not want to be.

Foy stopped smiling. He was tired of the hedges, tired of the whole bit. But what would happen when he told Jane?

He ducked the thought. Something might happen. Something would happen. He didn't like getting involved in messes. Better to wait and see.

The smooth, golden blond boy nodded familiarly to Hodges, the Wales family's elderly butler — older, possibly, than the hedges — who answered the door.

Hodges betrayed no surprise at the sight of someone dressed in a long robe painted with magic symbols, carrying a necromancer's hat under one arm.

"Miss Jane will be right down," said Hodges. He led Foy at a stately pace past several hangar-sized formal rooms to a small, comfortably shabby living room at the back of the house. Jane's mother, an older version of Jane, in worn, comfortable bathrobe and slippers, was watching TV, flipping the channels with her remote, and trailing the sash of her bathrobe for the cat.

"Mr. Foy," Hodges said, and withdrew.

"Foy," said Jane's mother, beaming. "Now, who are you supposed to be? Let me guess . . . Dracula?"

Above, at the top of the stairs, Jane stopped and watched the top of Foy's head go by. She looked at herself in the mirror. Dorothy in *The Wizard of Oz*.

Was it too juvenile — her brown hair in pigtails, the little stuffed toy cairn terrier in the basket over her arm? But she hadn't been able to resist the ruby slippers — exact copies of the ones in the movie.

She liked the idea. Being able to follow a yellow brick road anywhere it might take you. Making friends with scarecrows and lions and tigers.

Plain rhymed with Jane. Cyndi said anybody with money could look good. But Jane wasn't so sure. She thought, privately of course, that Cyndi just liked the way money looked.

Charity Webster said Cyndi's best color was the color of money.

She'd said it to *Cyndi*.

Jane had been paralyzed. And disgusted with herself for being so taken aback by an only slightly escalated version of the usual dialogue between the two.

But Cyndi, after a slight pause, had lifted an eyebrow and said, "Oh, yes, your parents are artists, aren't they?" and turned languidly away.

And Char had said, "And you're a piece of — art."

Char was outspoken, but not usually in a mean way. Cyndi had a knack for bringing out the worst in people somehow. And, somehow, it made her powerful.

I'd like some power, thought Jane. I'm tired of being in Kansas. What I need is your basic tornado. "Some action, baby," she said aloud, and then rolled her eyes at herself.

I will have a good time, she thought determinedly.

She looked down.

I will, I will, I will. She clicked the heels of her ruby slippers together three times. Then she skipped quickly down the stairs.

Rick Carmack was pleased with his costume. It had the maximum shock effect. Even his old man had flinched a little when he first saw it, before deciding on the indulgent smile bit.

"What'sa matter, Father? Never seen any blood before?"

His father kept that automatic smile on his face.

Like a permanent grimace. It probably came with being a mortician. No, not pc. The politically correct title was funeral director.

Right.

Now his father was sort of the McDonald's of the funeral business. A BMIG — Big Man in the Graveyard.

The whole thing made Rick nervous.

Everyone thought he was a big jokester. A party animal. If only they knew the truth. Rick was afraid of being still for even one minute.

When he'd been a kid, he'd even been afraid to go to sleep.

Because being still meant being dead.

And Rick had had his fill of death.

Moving at his usual top speed, Rick bounded toward the front door.

"Happy Halloween, Richard." His father's voice sounded behind him.

"I'll give my regards to the dead," answered Rick as he slammed the door.

Wills was annoyed. Annoyed that he'd agreed to double with Dade and Cyndi. Annoyed that he'd agreed to let Dade drive his big old Chevy. Annoyed with being upstaged.

Trust Dade to upstage everybody, he thought, slamming the car door shut behind him.

As if he'd read Wills's mind, Dade glanced over and surveyed Wills's costume. "Very original, Wills."

"At least people will know I'm Freddie Krueger," Wills said, and then was annoyed that he let Dade know he was annoyed.

"So right for you, Wills. But let me introduce myself — his Lord Highness Death — that's Mr. Death, to you."

Forcing himself to smile, Wills said, "Freddie Krueger and Mr. Death. We're kind of working the same side of the street, wouldn't you say?"

Dade nodded. "And this is Mr. Death's favorite holiday."

"Freddie's too," said Wills. "You know what, we should've borrowed my father's 'Lac."

"Mr. Death and Mr. Krueger cruising in a Cadillac. I like it. But I promised the All-American Metal Machine, since it's been such a good vehicle all year, that it could go out for Halloween."

"Hey, listen," said Wills, "it is no secret you are unnaturally attached to a jacked-up Chevy."

"Mr. Death warns Mr. Krueger to watch his mouth," said Dade.

"Really," said Wills. He wanted to say, who do you think you are? My family can trace its roots back to the Mayflower. Your aunt may be a local personality, but who the hell are you? Maybe you're not even an orphan. . . . Maybe she's not really your aunt. . . .

But he didn't.

Instead, he wished that his costume was real. He'd like to do a Freddie Krueger on Dade. Just to start.

Or a Jack the Ripper. He'd almost come as Jack the Ripper.

He *admired* Jack the Ripper.

A man after his own heart. Stalking the streets of London in the 1800s. Laughing at the cops. Keeping an entire city locked up in a nasty box of fear. Making people pay. . . .

He looked over at Dade broodingly. Dade could be unpredictable. Not safe to confront. Better to get him from behind.

Aloud he said, "Really," again. With an edge.

"Really," said Dade, turning into Cyndi's driveway. "Because Mr. Death, by virtue of who he is, isn't afraid of dying. But Mr. Krueger still has that option."

* * *

Jones was ready for the dance early. His costume consisted of putting on a cowboy hat. The rest already matched.

And the hat was real, too. He'd picked it up along the way. More or less honestly.

It would do for Halloween — this Halloween, here and now.

He closed the door of his dark house without saying good-bye to anyone. His car, battered and nondescript and made, lots of it, out of pieces of other cars, cranked to life with a mega-horse roar.

Appearances could be deceiving.

Important to always remember that.

Forgetting could be dangerous.

Believing what you thought you saw could be fatal.

He drove slowly down Main Street, a street lined on either side with small, expensive versions of the larger, expensive shops in the city. Charming town. Quaint. Well-preserved. The foot of the street ran into a dock from which whaling ships had once set sail. At the end of the dock you could look far out into the deep, calm harbor, held between the land on one side, and the long, curving point on the other that gave the town its name.

The tip of the Point was blunt, worn down by the ocean pushing against it, trying to get into the bay. Beyond the Point, a row of rocks, randomly visible, pitched up out of the ocean floor.

Sometimes you could see lights out there, they

said. Long-lost ghost ships that'd once sought the safety of the harbor and been caught by devilish mists and treacherous curling tides and renegade waves — and the rocks.

The Devil's Teeth, they called them. In the old days, people used to scavenge the Point for what washed ashore. And bury their dead there.

Jones glanced out to the Point as he turned and headed for the school. The moon was beginning to rise, laying a path straight across the dangerous waters. Cemetery Point. Once upon a time, and long ago, before the town had become a playground for the rich, that's what the whole town had been called.

The town had a past.

But then, what didn't?

In the school parking lot he pushed the car into a good spot in the shadows at the edge and kicked back to reconnoiter. A few people had already begun to drift into the gym for the Halloween dance, the chaperones and the wannabes, mainly. They'd all be at the dance, of course. But the dance wasn't the thing. Cyndi Moray's party afterwards was what really counted — trendy Cyndi and her too-cool-to-live friends.

He tapped his foot impatiently, scanned the darkening sky. A full moon was going belly up over the roof of the old school. Jones frowned. The old roof, bronzed to green with age (like everything else in this town, he thought) nevertheless gave off a pinkish, coppery glow from the metal beneath, picking up the lights in the parking lot that were beginning to flicker on. And the moon, rising above the Gothic, steeply pitched roof, looked for a moment as if it had caught on a sharp corner, as if the pink color were being drained out of it, to bleed down the roof, down across the building, down across the night. Spooky.

It was unseasonably warm.

"The sulfur fires from the other side," Jones said aloud, and then was annoyed with himself. He didn't like emotion. Feelings caused trouble. They caused you to imagine things: to imagine that you were in love. To imagine that you were loved. To imagine that you were safe. To put another person ahead of yourself.

No.

He would do what he had to do, and then he was out of there. History. Let him be somebody's past.

And somebody else's future.

He shifted in his leather jacket, crossed his cowboy-booted legs on the dash above the glove compartment, punched some heavy bass into the state-of-the-art sound system he'd soldered in under the dash.

He didn't like this night. Didn't like anything about it.

It was always tough being the new kid in town.

Charity Webster was getting ready in the midst of half a dozen siblings of varying degrees of relationship.

"I'll just be a minute, dear," their mother had said vaguely, heading out the door toward the car. The minute had been over an hour. Charity shook her head, smiling. If her mother didn't come back soon from wherever she'd gone, Char would have to think of something — or someone — to step into the baby-sitting breach. Not her stepfather. He was even more vague than her mother. He'd probably wonder where all the kids came from, if he noticed them at all.

He probably wondered how they'd gotten there in the first place.

"Char, Char," squealed her youngest brother.

"What, baby?" she asked, concentrating on making her face pale, pale.

"NOT a baby," he said. He paused. "What are you?"

"A witch," said Char.

"*Oooooh* a witch," screamed five-year-old Kim. The others took up the cry. "Oooh, ooh, a witch, a witch!"

She'd gotten them all ready for trick-or-treating earlier: a collection of ghosts in various colored sheets, with wonderful designs painted on them. That was one of the bonuses of having parents who were artists. And who knew — the sheets might become artworks someday and sell for millions.

In her dreams.

"A *good* witch," Char said, and stepped back to admire the results. Another decent thing about having artistic parents was the scope of their wardrobe. Somewhere it was written: Artists shall wear strange and sexy clothing.

Char was in a very unwitchy black Lurex bodysuit, with a short sequin tunic over it. She'd painted her unearthly red hair liberally with white, put on false fingernails of blood red.

She heard the kitchen door bang shut, and the music go on loud in the room her mother used as a studio. She smiled.

"Time for me to go, kids," she said. She picked up the towering witch's hat and placed it carefully on her head.

"Will you have fun?" asked Kim.

"Yes," said Char firmly.

And who knew? She might. Anything could happen. Who knew what the future would bring.

She *was* going to have a good time. Even if it killed her.

Chapter 2

"Look at the moon," said Jane. It was an unusually warm night for October, but the moon looked round and cool and seductive. Jane tilted her face back and closed her eyes. The moonlight painted the insides of her eyelids silver, making her see stars.

"Moonbathing?" Foy teased her.

She opened her eyes and grinned. That was the nice thing about being with Foy. He was so comfortable. You could say things like, "look at the moon," and he didn't think you were being corny and romantic.

On the other hand, a little romance wouldn't hurt. But Foy was not the one.

Foy took a sip from his flask, offered her some. She shook her head. He shrugged. When he'd had a little more, maybe he'd feel like moonbathing, too.

In the gym the dance was grinding on. Somewhere out there, up and down the pumpkin-lit streets of Point Harbor, the last of the trick or treaters were making their way home, wired out of their little minds on sugar and excitement. Foy sighed. He wished it were that easy to get out of *his* mind.

The back door to the gym opened and a blast of music poured out, bringing Dade Walken with it. Dade didn't wait for Foy to offer. He reached over and served himself from the silver flask Foy was holding. "Bad stuff," muttered Dade, wiping his mouth.

"Where's Cyndi?" asked Jane. Then she wondered why she'd asked. That was Cyndi, thought Jane disgustedly. Even when she wasn't there, people who didn't really want to know still asked where she was.

Dade looked at Jane and smiled slowly. She looked quickly away, feeling her face turn red. Good thing they were outside, in the dark. Or the relative dark. No one could see you blush in the dark, right?

"Moonburn?" said Dade softly, mockingly. Then he looked over at Foy. "Some party hat. Do you need one *that* big for your head? Who're you s'posed to be?"

Foy never let anything ruffle him. He wasn't about to let Dade start now. "Merlin. The magician."

Jane put in, "Mother thought he was supposed to be Dracula."

They all laughed. Then Dade said, unexpectedly, "Sometimes people don't make mistakes when they make mistakes, y'know?"

Shaking his head, Foy took another swig. "Oh, no, it's the Freud dude. Or Dade."

"It makes sense," said Jane. She met Dade's eyes again and forced herself not to look away. She had a moment of seeing him whole, his black shirt and black pants and black boots and long black cape, and the dark mask of pain on his face, a clock with thirteen numbers on it. The hands on the clock were painted so the clock was just about to strike thirteen.

Still holding Dade's eyes, she added, "And who are you supposed to be?"

Dade grinned, an evil, sexy grin. "Death, little Dorothy. As I was saying earlier to everybody's party object, Wills, it's Mr. Death to everyone else." He leaned forward and whispered in her ear. "But you can call me Death."

"This dance is dead!" Rick Carmack came briskly around the edge of the school. He was hyper, as usual. And as usual he was outrageous. Sometimes he was funny. Sometimes . . . not.

Jane checked out his costume and thought, euuww. But it fit him. His costume was classic Rick, just right: a psycho Santa Claus in a blood-spattered suit, holding a plastic ax.

"Where's our host?" Rick addressed Dade. "Cyndi's supposed to be meeting us here, isn't she? I mean, she did promise us a real Halloween party, right?"

On cue the door opened, and a group of people

came out. Cyndi, lethally attractive, had one hand on Wills's arm. Her other hand rested on the new guy's arm. Justin Jones. Only no one called him that.

Lara and Char were behind them, talking.

"You in costume, Jones?" asked Rick.

"Cowboy," said Jones laconically, touching his finger to his Stetson.

"Pretty lame," Richard shot back.

Jones shrugged as Lara drifted over to Wills.

"Is everybody ready?" said Cyndi.

"Trick or treat," said Rick. "Where is this party, anyway?"

"Don't be so pushy," said Cyndi, touching her tongue to the tip of each fang. "The trick will be to keep up with me. If you do, you get the treat."

She turned and headed down the stairs to the parking lot. Obediently, everyone else began to follow.

Beside Char, Jones said, "Do we trust her?"

"No," said Char.

Below, Cyndi turned. "Coming, Jones?"

Typical Cyndi.

Char stole a quick look at Jones. He was definitely worth looking at.

"We'll be right there, Cyndi," she answered.

The vampire teeth showed briefly in what wasn't a smile, then Cyndi whisked ahead to Dade's car. Jane looked back and gave Char a real smile. The rest of them, the Psycho Santa, the Freddie Krueger, the Rapunzel Princess, Merlin, floated fantastically beneath the distorting convergence of parking lot lights and moonlight and began getting into their cars.

And last but not least, a witch and cowboy followed them, all on their way to the real Halloween party.

The red lights ahead lurched crazily, righted, veered sharply left, and disappeared. Char looked over at Jones in the green glow from the dashboard.

"We're headed out to the old Point," she said. "Cemetery Point."

Jones looked back at her, his face unreadable in the dim light. "You scared?"

Char didn't know the answer, didn't want to tell him maybe yes. Instead, she said, "No one goes out there — comes out here — anymore. The road's been sealed off for as long as I can remember. They say it's dangerous, something about erosion and the tides. . . ."

"The road isn't sealed off now," Jones pointed out. Sure enough, just ahead, his lights picked out the huge metal gate, propped open in the barbed-wire fence. He eased the car through, and they caught sight of the taillights of Foy's car just ahead.

As the tires rasped over the metal grating beneath the gate, Char felt a thin shiver across her neck and shoulders, as if someone had laid a single burning finger against the nape of her neck. Almost without knowing it, she reached up quickly — just as Jones pulled his hand back.

"Don't do that," she said, and was surprised at the sharpness of her voice.

"You *are* afraid," said Jones. Then, softly, "That's okay. Being afraid's okay."

What a weird thing to say, she thought.

She frowned. He was new in school. From somewhere in the Midwest, he'd said. Ohio? Nebraska? Had he said exactly where? Maybe he hadn't. Come to think of it, he hadn't said much at all.

"Jones," she began.

"The one and only," he answered. "Listen. How long have you known Cyndi?"

Diverted, Char said dryly, "Too long."

"How long is that?"

"Only a guy could ask that question — let's see. My mother inherited our house here from her greataunt when I was seven. So ten years."

"Mmm," said Jones. "What about Rick?"

"Ten years," she said impatiently. "He was here when I got here, too. Jones, what about you?"

"What about me?"

"I've known you since school started. Or," she added hastily, "I've known who you are."

"Yeah?" he gave her a sideways leer.

"Well. You know what I mean. But, like, where are you from? What's the story?"

"Well, you know," said Jones conversationally, "I'm adopted. So I couldn't really say."

"Oh." She didn't know what to say to that. She studied Jones covertly. Who was he? She almost forgot, for a moment, the lurching car, the deeply rutted, nearly completely overgrown trail they were following, the signs that flickered from the twisted, salt-wind-stunted trunks of trees:

DANGER. NO TRESPASSING. GO BACK.

Go back?

No, that couldn't be.

"Did you see that?" she asked Jones.

He didn't answer.

Instead, he pulled the car to a stop in the thick darkness. Turned off the motor.

The thick, surging sound of the sea came crashing through the black velvet thickness of the night.

Her heart jumped. People got killed like this all the time. Didn't they? All he had to do was reach out, just like he had before. All he had to do was . . .

He turned toward her, as smoothly as a cat. She pressed back against the door, hard.

"J-Jones . . ."

He leaned toward her. Reached out.

"Jones, wait . . ."

And clicked the door handle. The door opened, almost tumbling her out to the ground, pulling him with her so he lay on top of her. They stayed still for a moment, balanced on the edge of the seat.

She felt her breath coming harder now, felt his breath against her lips. She lifted her face, felt his lips against hers.

Kiss me, kill me, she thought, half-angry with

herself for letting herself get so scared, half-amused at what a turn-on fear could be.

Was that what Jones had meant?

Was it fear — or pleasure — that was making it so hard to breathe evenly?

To breathe at all.

Whatever it was, it was working.

"Mmm," she murmured deep in her throat.

How long would she have stayed there in the weightless dark, a good witch being bad? And how bad . . .

She'd never know the answer.

Because a sound made her open her eyes. A wrong sound.

For a flash she couldn't focus.

And a flash was all it took.

The flash of moonlight on the blade coming down.

Chapter 3

Trying to scream. To warn Jones.

To twist out of the way.

Trying to close her eyes so she wouldn't see the ax when it came down on her face . . .

Screaming.

Screaming?

She wasn't screaming.

And then Rick was laughing above her.

"It's a trick ax," he chortled. "And you bought it." He laughed harder as Char and Jones pulled themselves out of the car. "Get it? You *bought* it!"

"Funny? *Funny?*" Char said. Her voice was a croak. "*Not*, Rick. No way."

"Every time you thump it against something, it makes that screaming sound," Rick went on, gleefully demonstrating again by whacking the side of Jones's car. "Sometimes I just *kill* myself."

Jones's hand shot out and caught the ax as Rick raised it again.

"Hey! Let go!"

"What're you gonna do, ax murder him?" Wills chortled behind them, silver moonlight flashing on the fake razor-blade fingernails as he made an elaborate show of slapping his hand against his thigh in amusement.

"Shut up, Willie," snarled Rick.

Wills said, "Watch it, Carmack."

"Or what? You'll rip me to death with your fingernails?"

"Lighten up, okay?" drawled Foy.

Char realized that everyone else had gathered around them — the whole sick-looking crew beneath the light of the moon.

Another shudder swept over her, and Jones's hand tightened on her hand. She looked down at his hand holding hers. When had that happened?

She looked over at him. His face was expressionless. He seemed cool, unfazed by the whole thing.

"Pretty decent joke," Rick insisted. "Admit it. You were scared witless."

"You wouldn't have the wit to know when to be scared," Jones answered evenly.

Rick snorted. "Deep. You're drowning us in it, Cowboy Jones."

Then Lara's voice broke through the tension. "Why are we standing around? This is a *party*," she said plaintively.

"You're right," said Dade. "Let's unload the cars. Wills, you and Richard carry the cooler. I'll be in charge of the music. Jones, get that box out of the trunk."

"I'll bring the blankets," said Foy.

"Why do we get stuck with the cooler?" Wills complained. "It weighs a ton."

"What'sa matter, Freddie, afraid you'll break your fingernails?" said Rick.

"Shove it," snapped Wills.

"Just do it, okay?" said Dade. He hoisted the boom box up on one shoulder, slung the CD case over the other.

"I'll come with you," Lara said to Dade.

"And why aren't the girls carrying something?"

"We're carrying the conversation," snapped Char, suddenly sick of the whole scene. Beside her, she sensed Jones's silent amusement.

"Where's Cyndi?" Jane intervened. I'm doomed, she thought. I'm doomed to keep asking the same dumb question. And I don't even want to know the answer.

Lara gave a little gasp. "Look!"

A tall figure in a clinging dress stood silhouetted against a dune just beyond the clearing where they'd parked their cars. Behind her, a faint path gleamed like an old scar in the scrub grass skirting the woods.

The figure beckoned sepulchrally.

"Yo, Cyndi," Rick called.

The figure beckoned again, then turned and glided into the darkness of the trees without answering.

"Creepy," said Lara. She put her hand on Dade's arm.

Wills snapped, "Pick up your end of the cooler, Carmack."

Rick smiled unpleasantly, but bent over and helped Wills hoist the cooler without comment.

"C'mon," said Dade. He nodded in the direction where Cyndi had disappeared. "Let's do like the lady wants."

Jane found herself looking at Charity.

Lady? thought Char as her eyes met Jane's. She raised her eyebrows at Dade's choice of words.

But no one was going to say the obvious.

"Yes," said Charity. "Let's do like the *vampire* wants."

Following the path into the woods, they wound in and out among the misshapen trees. Sometimes the path almost disappeared in the drifts of sand laying siege to the struggling trees. Sometimes the path was erased beneath the trees' gnomic moon-shadows.

"This is nothing but a big sand dune with trees," Wills panted.

No one answered. The wind kept up a steady keen, pushing clouds across the sky, blotting out the moon again and again, making the whole world flicker between darkness and light. And always, beneath the wind, the sound of the ocean could be heard, pounding and sucking against the shore and the ring of the Devil's Teeth beyond.

"Spooky," said Jones to Char in a conversational

tone, as if it were a sort of weather condition.

"Whose idea was this, anyway," complained Wills. "You were in on this, weren't you, Dade? How much longer do we have to walk?"

"Ah, you don't mind a little walk with Death do you, Freddie?" Dade's teeth flashed briefly. "And we got a cooler full of goodies so we'll all be nice and warm when we get there."

"It's really very warm for this time of year," said Jane. "Not cold at all." Then she thought, that's *it*. I get the stupid conversation of the year award. It's Halloween, and I'm talking about the weather.

Dade said, "See, Wills? A little walk with Death doesn't leave Jane cold."

"Just the opposite, sounds like," said Rick.

Wills said, "I wouldn't let Cyndi find out, Jane. She doesn't like to share."

"Low class, Wills," said Char.

"Oh, listen. Charity defends her *best* friend," Wills shot back sarcastically.

Lara said, "I don't think you should talk about Cyndi like that, Wills. *She* never talks about you."

Dade started to laugh.

And at last, the path opened up into another clearing. Only this one wasn't really a clearing.

It was the end of the trail.

They'd reached the tip of Cemetery Point. It was a high, rocky spit of land, pounded by the ocean on one side, gnawed by the currents on the other side where the water of the sound met the ocean. A crumbling stone wall enclosed the cemetery. Inside the wall, a crazy dance of weathered gravestones and monuments waited.

And just outside it stood Cyndi.

She turned and gestured grandly. Beyond her, where the graveyard began, was a huge pile of driftwood.

"Welcome to Cemetery Point," intoned Cyndi.

The moon went behind the clouds, and the rest of her sentence came hollowly out of the dark. "Happy Halloween."

They stood silently for a moment. Then, "Decent," Dade said, and went forward.

Wills and Rick followed to set down on the ground the cooler they'd been lugging.

"Let me do a little magic here," said Foy, dropping the blankets on the ground and kneeling by the driftwood. "Who's got some starter?"

Cyndi dropped to her knees beside Foy. "Yeah. I'd like that. C'mon and light my fire, Merlin."

"Here." Jane fished hastily in her basket and pulled a lighter out from under her stuffed Toto.

"The truth about Dorothy — she smokes," said Cyndi snidely. "Or is it only when you're not in Kansas?"

Jane felt her face flush in the darkness. It was my father's, she wanted to say. But why should she have to explain herself to anyone? Especially Cyndi.

Beside her, Char said, "Jane, I'll help you with the blankets," and bent to pick one up. Jane reached out gratefully to help her unfold it and start spreading it on the ground on one side of the bonfire.

The lighter flickered, and a moment later the fire leapt to life. The silvery darkness, the shadowed woods behind them, were obliterated by the brightness of it.

Dade set up the box on a level spot on the wall and cranked the music. Rick flipped back the lid of the cooler and said, "All *right*."

Finishing with the blankets, Char stepped back from the circle of firelight and turned. The grave-markers made her uneasy. Tilted at their crazy angles behind their low, crumbling stone wall, they seemed to be dancing in the erratic firelight.

"I don't know if this is a good idea," she said aloud before she could stop herself.

"So leave," said Cyndi. She put her hand on Dade's arm. "Dance," she commanded.

"All *right*," said Rick again, popping a top. "Let's party, animals!"

Wills threw his head back in a long, imitation werewolf howl.

"It'd be funny," Jones murmured, "if something howled back." He turned to Char. "Dance?"

A few minutes later, Char thought, I think this kind of dancing is probably illegal, or something. Because in spite of the chop beat of the music, Jones had wrapped his arms around her and was moving slow.

She pulled back. Felt, rather than saw him smile. They had danced to the edge of the circle of light, and she turned impulsively toward a gap in the crumbling wall.

"It's weird, this place," she said to Jones.

Following her into the graveyard, he said, "It's a graveyard."

"Yeah." She bent over, squinting at the words on the weathered stone and read, " 'Believed taken by the sea. May God have mercy on his soul.' "

"Sounds like there was some doubt about the mercy part," murmured Jones. "Maybe the drowning, too. . . ."

"He's buried *in* the graveyard," Char pointed out. "You can't get buried in a graveyard if you aren't, aren't . . . you know, if the church or whatever says it's not okay."

"Like suicides," said Jones.

"Right. That's still true, isn't it? If you commit suicide, then you can't get buried in holy ground, or something."

"For some churches," agreed Jones. "Look at this one: 'Borne on the tides up to heaven.' Kind of nice."

They wandered down the uneven row of stones. "These are all sailors, I guess." Char leaned over the wall to study a lone stone, all worn at the edges. "No, wait — look at this: 'Asleep but not at rest. May death bring her peace.' What does *that* mean?"

"I don't know. What do you think it means?" Jones caught her hand and began to walk back alongside the wall toward the fire.

"Sounds like she got zombie-ized."

Jones looked back, then slid his hand up Char's arm. "Zombi-ized?"

"Mm," she said, forgetting about the tombstone.

Then, for the second time that night, she forgot to think at all.

And just beyond, the music cranked on, and the clouds kept tearing up the moonlight, and everyone kept drinking and dancing and partying. As they came together and danced apart, they made long, strange shadows that leapt and twisted and merged with the shadows beyond the fire.

Jane sat down while Foy wandered over to the cooler where Rick was leaning on the wall, his long legs dug heel-first into the ground. Rick was drinking a lot, but, so far, thought Jane, it hadn't slowed him down.

"Are we having fun yet?" Dade left Cyndi digging through the cooler and walked over to squat down on his heels by Jane. He took a long drag on a cigarette, then snuffed it in the sand.

Jane took a hasty swallow of the warm beer she'd been holding all evening. "Yes."

"Then why aren't you dancing?"

She didn't answer for a moment. They watched the figures in the firelight making bizarre shadowy gyrations.

Wills had come up to Cyndi. He was saying something to her, too low to be heard across the fire above the music. Cyndi was looking up at Wills, a little smile on her face.

Dade followed Jane's gaze. He seemed amused. "Brave man," he commented.

"Does it bother you?" asked Jane impulsively.

"What?"

"About Cyndi and Wills. That he . . . you know, broke up with her, and she was so . . . so . . ."

"Unwrapped? Nah. Besides, there're at least two sides to every story. More, if you're dealing with creative people."

"I'm sorry," said Jane. "I shouldn't have asked."

"No problem. The problem is, why won't you dance with me?"

He caught Jane's hand and stood up, pulling her with him. At almost the same moment, Cyndi threw back her head and laughed. Then she turned and walked away from Wills and over to Rick.

The way she pulled Rick to her made Jones and Char look like the Bobbsey Twins.

Lara, who'd been standing nearby, started laughing.

Furiously, Wills whirled to face her. He raised his hand, and the shadows of his nails made stripes across Lara's face. For one awful moment, Jane thought he was going to lash out at her.

"Shrink's delight," said Dade, watching Wills.

Then Lara laughed again. "Freddie, Freddie, Freddie," she said delightedly.

And Wills slowly turned his hand over and bowed elaborately. "May I have this dance?" he asked.

"Sure," said Lara.

Jane started to dance with Dade, letting him spin her around and around in the firelight. Her dizzy eyes met Foy's once, briefly. He was smiling as if he enjoyed watching them.

34

But he wasn't enjoying watching half as much as she was enjoying the dance.

Jane had never danced with Dade before. It made her uncomfortable, to stand so close to him. Uncomfortable. Scared. Excited.

Dade was not a too-right guy. Everyone knew that. He was dangerous. There were rumors of drugs and fights and marathon parties where all the other partyers were left low and in trouble, only Dade still standing, able to move out of harm's way.

Some people said he carried a gun.

But no one knew for certain.

She liked that.

A sarcastic voice cut in on her dance. "Well, if it isn't little Dorothy. Close to Death."

The glitter in Cyndi's eyes was unmistakably menacing.

For a moment, Jane was almost afraid. Then, before she could stop herself, she laughed.

"What's so funny?" said Dade, swinging her away from Cyndi and Rick.

Away from harm, and looks that could kill.

"Nothing," said Jane. Her eyes met Char's and Char knew they were thinking the same thing: If Dade didn't carry a gun, having Cyndi around was probably the next best thing.

Char let Jones pull her down to sit beside him on one of the blankets. And Cyndi imperiously grabbed Rick's hand and swept through the gap in the stone wall and into the graveyard.

"Hey!" said Rick.

Cyndi turned. "Lift me up," she said.

Rick bowed. "As you vish, my beautiful vampire." He lifted Cyndi up. Then she got carefully to her feet on top of a low marble crypt. Rick scrambled up beside her. She pulled him to her, her arms locked just below his waist, and began to sway.

"C'mon," she called. "C'mon!"

Stupidly, Jane said, "You shouldn't do that, Cyndi."

"Shouldn't I? Shouldn't I? Who asked you?"

"Cyndi, come down," said Lara.

"You come up," replied Cyndi. "There's plenty of room."

But they all stayed where they were, staring up at Cyndi. The music cranked on. Cyndi and Rick kept dancing, their shoes scraping a protest out of the worn stone.

"What's the matter?" Cyndi taunted. "Afraid of a few dead people? Listen to the *truth*! This is the first party they've had in an eternity. They're happy."

Rick hooted. "Yeah. Grateful. The Grateful Dead, get it!"

"That sucks, Carmack," shouted Wills.

The wind gave a howling gust.

Something crashed in the trees behind them.

Lara was the first to begin to scream.

Chapter 4

"I bet they can hear you all the way back in Point Harbor. What's all the screaming about?" Georgina Butler made her entrance, strolling with studied nonchalance out of the dark fringe of the trees and into the firelight. In spite of the Halloween costumes, it wasn't hard to read the reactions: Jane, looking just like Dorothy, her eyes wide; Char, half-amused; Lara, faintly surprised and a little puzzled. All the guys, Georgie decided, looked appreciative.

But it was Cyndi's face, Georgie concluded, that made it worth the trip. Her eyes had narrowed to furious slits.

And as Georgie's date walked out of the shadows behind her, Georgie watched Cyndi's lip curl into a snarl. "*You*," she hissed, looking past Georgie. "What are *you* doing here?"

Cyndi Moray's brother, Dorian, walked up beside Georgie and put his arm around Georgie's shoulders.

Georgie looked around innocently. "We're not

late, are we? I mean, it won't be midnight for a while yet."

"Hey, Dade," said Dorian. He nodded offhandedly. "Any brew?" He went over to the cooler and began to study its contents.

"What're you doing here?" repeated Cyndi furiously.

"Dorian invited me," said Georgie, smiling.

"And I invited myself." Dorian reached into the cooler, helped himself, then turned to face his sister. "I figured you'd just forgotten."

The fact that Cyndi was dressed as a vampire and Dorian was dressed as a pirate didn't hide their similarities. They both were striking people, with high-boned cheeks and golden hair and enormous self-assurance. But Cyndi's costume was provocative, outrageous. Dorian was conservative and elegant in an authentic-looking costume, like the well-dressed captain of a pirate ship — with a hook for a hand.

Wills was scowling.

Rick looked over and smiled. "What'sa matter, Wills? Hook envy?"

"Shut up," said Wills, loathing in his voice.

But the loathing was nothing to match the loathing emanating from Cyndi and Dorian toward each other. Pure hatred.

Char, looking at them now, both of them giving off such a shimmer of angry heat that it seemed to dim the fire, thought it might be because they were so much alike. And both of them couldn't be the center of attention at the same time.

Cyndi and Dorian might have stood there in a frozen mutual hatred staring contest for eternity, but the music clicked off.

As Dade headed over to it, Rick said, "Leave it, Walken."

"Yeah?" said Dade.

"Yeah. Let's do something different."

Georgie looked at Cyndi and said sweetly, "I love games. Is that what you had in mind? Pin the tail on the donkey?"

That got Cyndi's attention. She looked away from Dorian, smiled suddenly at Rick, tilting her head slightly in Georgie's direction. "No, I have an idea, Rick. Since we have such a *special* guest. Why don't you just play the game you usually play with her. Hot potato, is it?"

Wills laughed, although no one else did.

Rick said, "How about ghost stories?"

"No way!" cried Lara, looking enthusiastic. "Do you know any good ones, Rick?"

"Naturally. Unless everyone else is" — Rick looked around the circle of faces — "chicken."

"Let's do it," Charity heard herself say, and she found herself sitting abruptly down on the ground, pulling Jones down with her.

He gave her a little smile, and said softly, so only she could hear, "Let's."

Char looked at him out of the corner of her eye,

then turned back to the fire as Cyndi slid down off the crypt. "Okay," Cyndi said. "We'll tell ghost stories. You go first, Rick."

One thing about Cyndi, thought Char, she never admitted defeat. Now she was taking charge of the ghost stories as if they'd been her own idea. And taking charge of Dade and Rick at the same time.

Georgie didn't like it. But she contented herself with snuggling up close to Dorian as they sat down by the fire across from Cyndi.

When everyone else had gotten comfortable, Rick leaned forward and gave the fire a poke. The flames shot up, and smoke rolled in ghostly clouds into the dark. Then Rick lowered his voice:

"Once upon a time, a couple went out parking on a dark, dark dead end road. . . ."

I've heard this one a million times, Char thought. This is so Girl Scout camp.

But she felt a faint thrill of fear in spite of herself. Maybe not the best place to tell ghost stories, thought Char wryly. Next door to a graveyard on Halloween. She glanced again at Jones. He was looking at Rick, his face expressionless.

Char wondered if her own face was as noncommittal. I don't like that graveyard, she thought. Then she thought, you're being stupid, Char. Everyone there has been dead and gone since the turn of the century. They have nothing to do with you. Nothing.

And there's no such thing as a ghost.

Foy had settled down by Jane. He was holding her hand in an absentminded way. Jane's attention didn't seem too fixed, either. She kept looking down, glancing sideways, shifting restlessly.

Is Jane spooked, too? wondered Char. And what is Foy thinking about? What does he see, staring at nothing like that?

Good thing we're not playing Truth or Dare.

Jane and Char hadn't been friends that long. They'd first started talking in art class their freshman year. The art teacher had been praising Char's neat, skillful, lifeless sketches. "Excellent technique," the old wannabe had been saying, and Char had been torn between feeling sorry for him and angry. She knew it wasn't her work he was praising, but her genes — her mother's, anyway.

Then she'd reminded herself, isn't this why you took the course? You knew it'd be an ace.

The teacher had paused again, and frowned. "Really," he had said reprovingly to the student whose sketches were scattered across the table.

When he'd moved on, Char had leaned over. The technique wasn't great, but the imagination was.

"Geez," she'd breathed. "You could really do it." Then she'd realized it was Jane Wales she was talking to. Jane, who didn't need to do anything for her whole life except live long enough to inherit the fortune her father had left in trust for her. Quiet, well-mannered, self-effacing, very rich Jane.

She'd expected Jane to smile politely and thank

her politely and that would be that. But Jane's pleasure had been real. And it had been the start of an unexpected friendship.

Quiet, well-mannered Jane. You wouldn't know she was restless unless you knew her.

Now Char caught another one of Jane's fleeting sideways glances. Dade.

Dade! thought Char. Maybe I *don't* know Jane.

Had Dade noticed?

More important, had Cyndi?

Char looked carefully in Cyndi's direction through the veil of her eyelashes.

Cyndi was tapping one vampire tooth with one long red nail, looking a little bored.

Don't let Cyndi see you, Jane, thought Char. 'Cause if she does, girlfriend, she'll have your blood.

Georgie's applause brought her back to the fireside abruptly.

Dorian said, "A tried-and-true story, Rick. The hook, the car door, the whole bit."

"But it's a great story, anyway," insisted Georgie.

"I like it," agreed Lara. "It's not so scary if you know how it ends."

"Hey, Jones," said Dade. "You got any stories?"

"Nothing you haven't heard," said Jones, his face unreadable.

"I've got one," Dorian cut in.

Without waiting for anyone else to speak, he began. "Once upon a time, there was a vampire. A vampire on wheels, if you know what I mean." His eyes locked with Cyndi's, and Georgie giggled.

"This vampire couldn't keep her teeth off other people's property. Or other people. She liked to take what wasn't hers. So she started getting fat. And then she couldn't catch the people anymore. So she had to go to this graveyard and suck on the dead people."

"Gross," cried Lara. "Isn't that gross?"

Cyndi, her eyes snapping with fury, said softly, "Boring."

"I haven't finished," her brother answered. He smiled, handsome like a golden cat warming itself by the fire.

"Anyway, our fat, greedy vampire, who was nothing but a big fake, because what self-respecting vampire would ever let this happen, made a big mistake. Because all the people in the graveyard weren't quite dead yet. One corner of the graveyard was for the undead. And she dug up one of the undead, and it was a vampire. And it bit her. And you know what happens when a vampire takes a direct hit from another vampire — at least what happens to a bogus vampire?"

"What?" Dade's voice was as soft as Cyndi's. But more frighteningly menacing, somehow.

Dorian seemed unaware of the menace. "Major, permanent bloodletting. Like she'd turned into a hemophiliac. Bleeding and bleeding. So the old vampire was freed, and this new, bloody, bogus vampire got buried in his grave. And she's there to this day, buried alive, too weak to leave. Her blood turning the whole earth around her red. And no one will save her because no one loves her. Or ever will."

"What's love got to do with it?" said Cyndi, her eyes on her brother.

"Disgusting." Lara shook her head. "All that blood."

Jones looked back and forth between them. Then he shook his head. "You guys go too fast for me."

"It's almost midnight," said Georgie. She lowered her voice at midnight. "Ooooooh."

Then she looked around the circle of faces. "I know. Let's all hold hands and see if we can contact the dead. You know, like a séance?"

"Anything to grab onto a guy's bod, Georgie?" Cyndi sneered.

"Afraid?" challenged Georgie.

For an answer, Cyndi grabbed Dade's hand and Jones's.

"Go for it, Georgie," said Dorian, sounding amused.

Jones frowned as the ring of people joined hands in a circle with the fire at the heart of it.

"This," Georgie intoned, closing her eyes dramatically, "is All Hallows' Eve. We call to you, spirits trapped beyond life. We call to you, spirits who wander the earth. We call to youuuu . . ."

Jones's hand twisted in Char's. She tightened her fingers unconsciously.

"Arise!" wailed Georgie, raising up her own hands. Everyone in the circle followed suit.

A blast of wind came out of nowhere, drowning all sound.

A log shifted on the fire, and a tongue of flame shot from the heart of the embers up into the night.

Jones said, "No!" and yanked his hands free, breaking the circle.

"Hey!" cried Georgie. "You ruined it!"

"Let's dance some more," Char said, jumping up. The night was getting too weird. In fact, it had been too weird all along. She thought, it's almost like, put people in disguise and their true nature comes out.

Then Char felt the whole Point tilt fractionally.

No one else seemed to notice. Looking sulky, Georgie was allowing Dorian to coax her into dancing. Lara had started laughing at something Wills had said. Jane and Foy bent over the box, fiddling with the sound. Rick finished chugging his beer, tossed the can over his shoulder, and began to follow the edge of the low wall into the dark, fumbling with his pants. Cyndi and Dade began to dance.

Char lost her balance.

She felt the tremor through her body, a shock and an aftershock.

Dark. Like pain. Pain remembered.

She looked at Jones.

"Jones?" she said.

He was looking at his hands.

"Jones," she said again. "Jones . . ."

"It's time to go," he answered at last, his voice low and urgent.

"You felt it, didn't you?"

"Now," Jones said. And grabbing her wrist in a vise of iron, he began to pull her into the darkness under the trees.

Chapter 5

"Where are you going?" Cyndi's voice cut across the blast of the music.

Everyone turned to look.

"A little Charity work, Jones?"

Char felt the angry heat in her face. She stopped and tried to pull free of Jones's grip.

He didn't let go.

Cyndi put her hands on her hips and smiled. Her vampire fangs glittered. So did her eyes. "Or just going to play a little hide-and-seek? What a *good* idea!"

Behind Cyndi the moon came out.

"I hate this," Jane said softly to Foy. "I wish whatever is going to happen would just *happen*." But she stayed still, waiting.

Everyone seemed to be doing the same thing. They all remained motionless, a game of statues.

Char took a deep breath. She looked past Cyndi, at the graveyard stretching into the shadows beyond where the real statues waited out eternity in memory of the dead.

Jones's hand tightened on her arm.

"What time is it?" asked Georgie, clinging to Dorian's arm.

Her question somehow diffused the moment.

With some difficulty, Dorian turned his wrist over so he could see his watch.

"Three minutes till midnight," he said.

"Excellent," said Cyndi. "When I clap my hands, all the girls can hide. Then I'll count to thirty, and the guys can come look for you."

"What does that make you, Cyndi?" asked Georgie. "One of the guys?"

Before Cyndi could answer, Dade raised his hands. "I'll put my hands together for you, Cyndi. Then you can hide, too."

Dade looked at Cyndi, who stared rebelliously back at him. Then, slowly, reluctantly, Cyndi climbed down off the tombstone.

"Wouldn't it be great to play hide-and-seek and let Cyndi hide forever?" muttered Georgie to Lara. But Lara was busy tucking her short gold hair beneath the long gold Rapunzel wig, and didn't seem to hear.

This time, the tremor was more distinct.

Char looked up at the sky. Although the wind was blowing strongly now, the clouds no longer whipped past the moon. It stood, frozen and alone in its nimbus of fiery light, like an eye in a socket of exposed bone.

This time, Char had felt the tremor through the soles of her feet, up her spine, into her heart.

"Jones?"

"Run," hissed Jones, releasing her arm, his voice as thin as glass.

She looked at his face. It was as bleached as the bone-socketed moon.

"Jones," she said again.

"Ready?" drawled Dade. He pressed his hands palm to palm and raised them high above his head.

"Run," said Jones. "Back to the car. Don't stop. Don't look back."

He gave her a push.

What about you? she wanted to cry. What about Jane? What about everyone else?

But suddenly a cloud came from nowhere, and she felt the earth pitch as if it were about to open and swallow her whole. Just before the moon was blotted out, she had a last glimpse of Dade, high on the crypt in his black-and-silver Death outfit, like a priest in some ancient, evil rite, his hands raised above his head. Like a prayer.

She didn't wait to hear him clap. She was running for the cover of the trees, each breath stolen from the fear that was choking her.

She'd never been so afraid in her life.

But, then, she'd never run for life.

Dade felt a gust of wind almost make him lose his footing. But he caught himself, quick as a panther. He raised his voice and began to count.

Below him, the guys lounged around, their eyes obediently sort of closed, while the girls scattered.

Dade kept counting. He kept his own eyes open. But he didn't watch anyone hide. Instead, he watched Char sprint into the woods. Something about the way she was running . . .

"Twenty-one . . . twenty . . ."

Dade let the pause draw out. This crypt gave you a pretty good view, he thought. He looked down at Foy and Wills and Dorian standing just below, with Jones a little ways beyond.

"Hey, Merlin, use your magic powers and tell me where they're hiding," he said to Foy.

Foy said, "Use your eyes. You haven't got them closed, have you?"

"Who told you?" said Dade, and began to count again.

"It's not fair," said Wills, opening his eyes and leaning over to give the fire a poke with one of his long, plastic-silver razor nails.

Dade said, "Be careful, my man. You'll melt your fingernails. Then we'll have to call you Freddie the unready. . . ."

"Pretty good, Dade." Dorian nodded.

And what are you doing here, college boy? thought Dade. Did you come all the way back to town just to give your sister a little Halloween surprise?

"Where's Rick?" asked Foy.

"I'll check," said Dade. "Twenty-two, twenty-three . . . RICK!"

"Yeah, yeah," a faint voice came back from a dark corner.

"Hey," called Dade, "you're not doing what I think you're doing on those graves, are you, Richard?"

A faint giggle came from another corner of the graveyard.

"What do you think?" Rick's voice was closer now, and in another moment he came into view, wrestling with the zipper on his Santa suit.

"You *are* a psycho Santa . . . twenty-four, twenty-five. Hey, Jones, no fair, getting a head start."

Jones didn't answer. He just stood there.

Dade took a swig from the flask. Oops. Almost lost his footing that time. Had to be careful on these crypts. "Twenty-six, twenty-seven, twenty-eight . . ."

"Just for the record, I plan on taking my time out there in the dark," said Rick, wiggling his eyebrows up and down maniacally.

"Twenty-nine . . . you don't have to spell it out for us, Rick. We'll figure it out . . . thirty." Dade raised his voice.

"Ready or not, here we come!" shouted Wills.

"Death's coming to getcha," Dade called. He leapt off the crypt with a flourish and headed into the darkness in the general direction where Cyndi had disappeared, ignoring the others.

What a creep joint, Dade thought, threading his way across the uneven ground, between the gravestones. And what happened to the moon?

"Cyndi," he said. He heard a faint noise to his left, and smiled. Cyndi was up to something. She always was. If she couldn't make trouble, she'd borrow it. He had pretty low expectations of anything between them. He smiled a different smile, thinking about some of their past dates. Very low expectations.

Cyndi smiled to herself. She'd found a hollow of ground beneath a broken-off monument. She was crouched beneath it. When Dade got closer, she was going to jump out and give him the scare of his hot-blooded, cold-hearted life. She could hear him now . . .

Or maybe it wasn't Dade. That was an interesting possibility, too.

Jane knelt down miserably in the shadows of the cold stones. She should've done what Char had done, and made a run for the woods. But none of them had, except Char. Maybe because Jones had been standing there.

Something about Jones. Something about this whole night.

A shadow passed. Dade?

Then she thought about all the shadows around her. Shadows of tombstones. Shadows of the dead . . .

Stop it, she told herself.

But why did they always end up doing what Cyndi wanted to do?

Foy gave his robe a yank. It kept catching on the underbrush. At least he'd dumped the hat. You could see that hat coming a mile away. He skirted the edge of the graveyard slowly. Up ahead, he thought he saw a figure crouched in the shadow of the crumbling stone of the graveyard wall. Yes.

Georgie peered cautiously over the top of the angel's half-furled wing. What a perfect hiding place. An angel. And speaking of angels, where was Jones? Or Dade? Wouldn't that put Cyndi in a twist? Her gaze swept the fire-lit clearing. But Jones wasn't standing there anymore. Had he headed toward the graveyard, instead of out into the woods after Char?

Stupid Charity. No one would ever find her in those woods. You'd need a bloodhound, or something.

Someone was coming. She slid back down.

Rick didn't care how much noise he made. It didn't matter who he found. Unless it was Cyndi, and she was feeling like making some trouble to pass the time. Which was not a bad idea. If he found Cyndi first, and she was glad to see him, it might be a little while longer before Dade found them.

And Dade wouldn't care. Would he?

* * *

Dorian found a flat, worn-down stone and sat down on it. He lit a cigarette. Waited. He wasn't about to go thrashing through or around a graveyard. He had better things to do.

Wills stumbled over something and cursed. Damn graveyard. Stupid game. He wrinkled his nose. Something stank. Then he saw the deeper shadow on the ground ahead of him. Had someone been digging? He stopped uneasily. Was that what smelled so bad? An open grave?

Then he remembered that the graveyard was long unused. Whatever had been buried wouldn't smell anymore.

Ugh. Maybe something had fallen in, an animal or something, and hadn't been able to get out. . . .

Stupid animal.

Something made William Lawrence Howell turn.

Something was standing behind him. Something big. Not the right costume. Not right. Not . . .

The moon came out.

He had a fraction of a second to see.

It wasn't what he expected.

The world tilted.

He threw up his hand in a futile gesture of defense. The shiny ends of silver-plastic razor nails flew through the air like bits of confetti.

The great glittering blade hooked him under the chin. It caught, fractionally. Wrenched sideways.

54

The boy dressed like Freddie was in shock long before it was finished.

He never knew he was dead.

Lara was getting bored. The people sneaking around the graveyard were making enough noise to wake the dead. Why hadn't anyone found her yet?

She waited a few seconds longer. An eternity. Then, with a little pout, she jumped to her feet from the edge of the raised gravemarker where she'd been sitting. The graveyard didn't really bother her. In fact, the raised grave had reminded her a little of those raised garden beds made with railroad ties that her older sister was always digging in. The smell of earth wasn't too different from the gardening center her family owned, either.

She sensed rather than saw a movement in the far back corner of the graveyard, where the wall had stopped. Or maybe it had crumbled down. Maybe there had been a wall, and they'd run out of room and had to bury people outside the wall.

It didn't interest her. It didn't really matter.

She raised the hem of her dress and walked lightly across the graves.

The moon came out suddenly. She saw something flash in its light. Wills's Freddie Krueger nails. It had been a pain trying to dance with him while he was wearing those things.

She heard a sound, sort of a muffled ripping sound, the way the wet packed earth sounded when her sister stuck the trowel in.

A wet, protesting sound.

"Wills?" she called softly, rounding the corner of the wall.

The wind had died, but the cloud-blotted darkness remained. Branches slapped her face. She'd lost the path. Dimly, Char thought, if I can just find the edge of the dune. If she could reach it, she could follow the dune's edge back to the clearing where the cars were parked.

"Here we come . . ." Dade's voice.

How long had she been running? Thirty seconds? A minute?

A lifetime.

She shoved the branches aside, peering ahead for the white glint of sand.

The dunes would be treacherous. Walking the edge of them would be like walking in quicksand on the edge of a cliff. To lose her footing would mean a steep fall to the rocky ledge of shore below. Although she'd never been there, she knew that somehow. Didn't have time to think how she knew.

She stopped to catch her breath.

And heard it.

Something was crashing through the woods behind her.

Jones, she thought.

But she didn't say it aloud.

Maybe it *was* someone playing hide-and-seek. One of the guys. Foy or Dade or Rick. Or even Lara or Jane or Cyndi or Georgie, looking for a hiding place.

Maybe.

She didn't move. Tried not to breathe. Crouched down now, hoping the moon would never come out to give her away. At least she was dressed in black. Witch's black.

If she were really a witch, she wouldn't be so afraid in the midnight darkness of Halloween. Why wasn't she a witch? A *bad* witch?

The crashing stopped.

With the cessation of sound, the darkness was complete.

Midnight.

She knew in her bones it was midnight now. High midnight on All Hallows' Eve on Cemetery Point.

Midnight only lasts a minute, she told herself. In one minute, it won't be midnight anymore. In one minute, it will be over.

And then the screams began.

There had never been such a sound. It went on and on. It spread out like a wave, drowning the night. It was raw and terrible. Inhuman.

Instinctively, Char put her hands over her ears. The sound came through, drove through her hands, into her senses. Into her brain.

She ran now, not caring what was behind her, not caring what was ahead. She ran blindly under the blazing light of the moon. She ran with her hands balled in fists, pressing them against her ears, punching her way through the trees.

Until something caught her by the ankle. And the darkness came up to meet her.

She was in the water. The water was warm. The waves had a friendly feel as they pulled at her ankles. As if they wanted her just to come in and play.

But who ever swam in the dark in the ocean? Things could get you. Sharks. Undertow.

Or worse.

She stood in the pull of the waves, the water swelling and pulling at her thighs, the long skirt of her dress twisting like seaweed around her.

Out beyond, the shadowy Devil's Teeth grinned jaggedly. Something was sailing there, just past them. Sailing in the dark and heaving waters, sailing safely among those teeth.

Something was hunting out there.

But she was waiting for it.

And then the water turned to ice around her thighs, and the wind laid cold wet hands against her cheeks and froze her breath, and she couldn't move.

It had come.

" . . . Char . . . Charity?"

"No one calls me Charity," she murmured, coming up out of the nightmare into the dark.

"Don't cry. It's all right."

"I'm not crying." But she was. She could feel the tears on her face, feel how cold they were.

And feel the hand there.

She opened her eyes. The moon was shining. She was lying in soft sand. The branches of trees were silhouetted against the sky above her.

"Can you get up?" A different voice. Familiar. But odd. Not right.

"Yes," she said.

"Let's get out of here," said another voice. Georgie's. Yes. Now Char remembered. She'd been running. Someone had screamed.

They'd been playing a game.

"Is the game over?" she asked.

No one answered. Instead, hands were hauling her to her feet.

"Lean on me," said a voice.

"I'm fine," she said, suddenly indignant.

She began to make her way carefully toward the cars. Someone stepped ahead of her and opened a door. Other figures hurried by her in the silver light. Grotesque figures — Santa Claus and a spider woman and Captain Hook . . . all scurrying, scrabbling.

Halloween. That's right, it was Halloween. That was Jones. And Jones's car.

She put her hand on the car door and looked across the top of the car at Jones. "What happened?" she asked.

"For God's sake, get in the car," someone snarled behind her. She was pushed unceremoniously in. The door slammed behind her. More people piled into the back seat. Jones started it up, slammed it to reverse, turned it around.

Behind them, other cars followed.

Jones drove fast, lurching in the overgrown sand track, scraping against trees. Grabbing the dash to keep her balance, Char turned to look back.

The clearing was empty.

In the seat behind her, outlined in the headlights of the car behind them, sat Lara and Cyndi and Dade.

"Where's Jane?" she asked.

Cyndi answered. "In one of the other cars. Foy's."

"What about . . ."

Cyndi cut her off. "Georgie Porgie is with Dorian, okay? And Rick is probably with them, if he isn't with Foy."

"But what about Wills?" Char looked at Lara. Lara didn't answer.

Char faced Jones. "What's going on? What happened? Is the party over?"

"You could say that," said Jones. He accelerated through the open gate and down the narrow track to the road.

"Where's Wills?" said Char.

"Dead." Cyndi's voice, hoarse and ragged, pulled Char's attention back. The vampire fangs flashed briefly, uselessly, in the dark, as Cyndi licked her lips carefully.

"He's dead," she repeated.

Chapter 6

"Dead." said Char.

Lara turned her head away. Cyndi stared defiantly back at Char.

Dade said, "Yeah."

For the first time, Char noticed the dark stains on Lara's pink princess dress.

It can't be blood, she thought.

They were on the beach road now, twisting and turning back to Point Harbor.

"This is a joke," said Char. "A bad Halloween joke. Cyndi — "

But whatever she'd been about to say, telling Cyndi it wouldn't work, that Cyndi wasn't going to get away with this kind of garbage, was cut off by Jones's voice.

"He was ripped up pretty bad."

"How do you know?" asked Cyndi sharply. Then, "That's right. You stayed. You stayed and *looked* at him."

Dade spoke just as sharply. "Better than running away."

Cyndi jerked away from him and sat rigidly on the seat between Dade and Lara.

"He was on the ground." Jones's voice was flat. "Lara was over him, screaming. I pulled her away and tried to see if he still had a pulse or anything."

Lara's voice, as flat as Jones's: "He was still moving. . . ."

"Sometimes that happens, even after . . . after a person is dead."

"How do you know so much, Jones?" Dade's voice was curious, as if they were discussing a theory, not someone they knew. "Rick knows that kind of stuff, probably, 'cause of his father. Wills was a specialist in it, but then he wasn't wrapped right."

"Stop it! *What happened?*" Char almost screamed.

The lights of Point Harbor came up to meet them. The streets were almost empty now. But jack-o'-lanterns still burned in the windows, silhouettes of construction paper skeletons and cats and pumpkins still decorated the windows. One of the houses had been rolled. Toilet paper fluttered in the branches like shredding flesh on twisted bones. Someone had, as usual, poured soap into the fountain in the center of town.

Jones turned down the street by City Hall. Turned again and slid the car to a stop outside a low, quiet, brightly lit building.

"The police station!" said Cyndi.

Lara's voice, flat expressionless: "Of course it is, Cyndi. What did you expect? We have to report a murder."

"She's expecting me."

Hodges hesitated, then Jane said, behind him, "It's okay, Hodges."

He gave a stiff nod and stepped aside and Jane hurried forward to seize Char's arm. "Oh, Char, I'm so glad you're here. I couldn't sleep."

They'd been at the police station until almost dawn. As they'd left, Char had looked out toward Cemetery Point. Yes. Searchlights. No one had believed them at first. But they'd believe them now.

Only she still wasn't quite sure what had happened.

"Come up to my room. Would you like something to eat? Oh. I guess that's not . . ."

"It's okay, Jane." Char followed Jane up the stairs to her big, immaculately kept corner room. Every light in it was on. All the windows had the curtains pulled back as far as they would go.

"No wonder you couldn't sleep." Char tried to make a feeble joke, motioning toward all the light.

"I didn't want to be in the dark," said Jane simply.

Char sat down in one of the small, down-filled chairs and leaned back wearily. She was exhausted. But she hadn't been able to sleep, either. Jane's phone call had been a welcome relief.

She watched as Jane fidgeted: flopping back across her bed, sitting up, rolling over on her stomach, and pulling a pillow under her chin.

Jane was normally so calm. Normally.

Normal.

We won't be using that word for a while, thought Char. Because what had happened — whatever it was — was definitely not normal.

Jane pulled a tendril loose from her tightly drawn-back brown hair and began to inspect the ends. One foot bobbed up and down over the far edge of the bed.

Not normal. Wills was dead.

"Who?" said Char aloud. "And why?"

Jane got still. She looked at Char, her eyes huge. "It was one of us. Wasn't it?"

"I didn't say that. It could have been some random person out there. Some bum, maybe."

"Yeah," Jane responded lukewarmly, her eyes still fixed on Char's face. "Yeah. Some bum who just happened to walk all that way out to Cemetery Point, and was waiting there for us on Halloween."

"He — or she — could have been living there," Char pointed out. "Or it could have been some pinball crazy person who knew about the party and got there first. . . ."

"Or followed us out." Jane nodded slowly. "Like Georgie and Dorian."

"Yeah," said Char. She hesitated, then said, "Did you notice anything, Jane?"

"Like what? The police asked me that, too."

"I'm not the police."

"I know. It's just that . . . no. No. I don't remember much of anything. I mean it was spooky and all. It was so . . . so Cyndi to have that party . . . I mean, I didn't want to go in the first place. . . ."

"Yeah. I mean, I probably wouldn't have gone if Jones hadn't come along. I think I went with him just to yank Cyndi's chain."

Meeting Jane's level gaze, Char added, "Well maybe not *just* to yank Cyndi's chain." She almost smiled, remembering. Then she remembered the run toward the darkness, the panic like some uncut drug speeding through her veins on its way to stopping her heart, remembered the sound of Dade's voice behind her, counting down the mortal seconds.

Remembered the heaving earth beneath her feet.

"Details," said Char, coming back to the present. "Don't think about the whole thing. Just try to remember the details."

"Well . . ." Jane began slowly, and Char felt a surge of hope. Although what exactly she hoped for, she didn't know.

"I know the way, don't worry," a voice sounded in the hall. A moment later, Jane's door opened.

"I thought *you'd* be here," said Cyndi, by way of acknowledging Char.

The three of them looked at each other in silence. Then Jane said to the flustered-looking maid who had appeared behind Cyndi, "It's okay. Thank you."

Cyndi didn't look good, thought Char. But, then,

who did? She'd washed the witch's paint off her face, removed the red talon press-on nails from her fingers. But vestiges of paint still clung to her skin, and she hadn't had time to wash the white paint from her hair, only to comb it so it at least wasn't spiked straight up.

Cyndi was pale, almost as pale as her vampire makeup had been. Traces of black liner still ringed her eyes, and her mouth looked chapped at the corners where the vampire teeth had rested.

Without waiting to be invited, Cyndi dropped into the other chair and pulled her feet up under her. As usual, she was all in black. It didn't fit in Jane's blue-and-ivory room.

"Cyndi?" asked Jane.

"Jane?" mocked Cyndi.

Char felt her temper rise. It was just like Cyndi to walk in and muddy the waters. That girl was a walking personality disorder.

"We were talking about the murder," Char said sharply. "It kind of ruined your party, didn't it?"

Cyndi said, "Yeah. I guess you could say the murder spoiled all the fun."

"Fun," repeated Char neutrally.

But Cyndi didn't rise to the bait. "I thought you'd be here," she repeated. "Both of you. That's why I came."

"Why?" said Jane.

"Because Wills is dead. And maybe someone might think . . . might think it was my fault."

Jane gasped.

"Is it?" asked Char, watching Cyndi closely.

"Char!" exclaimed Jane.

"It's okay. You're a . . . witch, Char, but you're consistent. I . . . in a funny way, I trust you."

"I'd stick to trusting my friends," muttered Char.

Cyndi hunched one shoulder in a contemptuous shrug. "Friends," she said.

"But Lara," began Jane.

"Home. Doing the grief number. With the help of the doc's prescriptions."

"And you're here," said Char.

Cyndi said to Jane, "You see what I mean about Char?" To Char she said, "And I'm here."

"Why?"

With some difficulty, Cyndi said, "Because the cops think I set the whole thing up: the party, the games . . ."

"The murder," said Char.

"To get even with Wills. To pay him back for us splitting. Someone told them all about it."

"I didn't," said Jane.

Cyndi said, "I know. And I know Char didn't, either."

Jane frowned.

Cyndi said, "You wouldn't. People like you, Jane, don't gossip. To the cops or anybody. You live in a closed circle. You protect what's in it. You don't talk about what's outside it.

"And Char wouldn't because she doesn't like me. It's sort of like a weird code of honor. Am I right?"

"I didn't say anything to the cops," said Char.

Cyndi smiled. "That's the difference between you and me, babes."

"Everyone did know about you and Wills," interceded Jane. "He — they — said you'd had a big fight."

"He said it," said Cyndi. "He told everyone his version. He had a big mouth. Big man. Big stud. He didn't get it, you know? All he wanted was to be somebody famous, even if it was only for fifteen minutes. And even if it was only for going out with me."

Char said, "You were just using him, too."

"So? I'm not on this earth to fall in love, get married, and have babies. . . . And, anyway, it was mutual. I just wish I'd dumped him first. I could've killed him for that."

Her words hung in the air.

Cyndi smiled.

"Jeez," muttered Char.

Cyndi said, "I could have killed him, but I didn't. I've got to prove it.

"And the only way to prove I didn't kill Wills is to find out who did."

Chapter 7

Jones was thinking about murder.

How easy it was. How people got away with it.

On TV. In films.

In real life.

Sometimes it was hard to remember what was real. Sometimes it was hard not to believe what wasn't.

Nothing seemed real.

Maybe being dead was what was real. Maybe that was the only reality.

"Heavy," muttered Jones disgustedly.

He was sitting at the overlook by the Back Bay Road. He'd been there all night. Had watched the sun come up over Cemetery Point.

On the previous night, what was left of Halloween night, lights had glimmered and flickered until dawn out on the Point. But last night, it had been dark and still, lit only by the waning moon.

The sunrise had been spectacular, a definite ten for special effects: the sky shot full of colors, a decorator's nightmare, turning the Point gray, then silver, then blood red.

The cops would have the Point roped off. Scene of the crime.

On the Bay Road behind him, the Point Harbor morning traffic had begun — six or eight cars.

Why would anyone live in a place like Point Harbor?

Crazy to live that way.

Unreal crazy.

Almost as crazy as murder.

Another car. This one didn't pass by. It pulled to a stop behind him.

He watched it in the rearview mirror. Watched the driver get out and saunter toward him.

The door on the passenger side of his car opened. Dade slid into the seat next to him. Looked out at the view.

"Say you wanted to off someone," Dade said conversationally. "How would you do it?"

Char was dreaming again. She knew she was dreaming. She knew the dream. She'd been there before, that night on the Point when she'd been running away from Cyndi's party.

This time, she wasn't in the water. This time she was on the dunes above, looking out to sea. Although the moon was waning, the Devil's Teeth glistened with an unholy light: the carnivorous smile of the sea.

The somber, heavy wool dress she was wearing

didn't warm her. She was cold to the heart.

But he was there. Out there. Waiting. Waiting for her to call him to her. They would say she had a demon lover. But it wasn't that.

Because he had taken everything that she had loved, everything that ever mattered. And that had changed her.

She felt the power rising through her veins, more scalding than any passion, more dangerous than any love. Immortal power.

She didn't know where it came from. Or why.

She didn't care anymore.

Whatever it was, whatever he was, she would kill him. And if he would not die, well, then, it would be a fight beyond death.

She would wear out eternity before she rested.

Raising her arms, she began to call him to her.

Char woke. Her arms were raised, as if she wanted to pull the darkness to her and hold it tight.

Like a lover.

No.

No.

She jerked her arms down, scrabbled in the blankets, and pulled them up over her head as if she were a child again.

What was happening to her?

Why?

She had to stop it. She had to fight it.

She was afraid.

The cold cut her to her bones. Mortal fear.

"I'm not afraid of dying," she whispered in the blanket darkness.

I'm not afraid of dying.

I'm afraid of something worse.

Lara slept on. She'd always liked to sleep. Slept liked the dead, her family said.

Sleeping was one of the things Lara did best.

But she'd had trouble sleeping after Wills's death. Even with the 'scrip to calm her down. So the doctor had phoned another 'scrip into the pharmacy, and the pharmacy had delivered it.

And if the dead slept without dreams, without memories, without moving, then Lara was sleeping the sleep of the dead.

"Yo, Father," Rick had said. "A little business for you. Sort of makes us a team, right?"

His father had looked away.

Rick had almost felt bad.

But he'd asked anyway: "Are you gonna be the one who — makes Wills into a beautiful memory picture?"

"The family has contacted us," his father had said.

Rick had felt bad then, a little. Bad and weird.

So he'd said, "Well, you've got your work cut out for you. Get it?"

After leaving the police station, Dorian had sacked it for the day. He got up Sunday evening to find the house empty except for servants. And his sister.

He didn't see her at first. He'd wandered into the library to scrounge in the bar. Something had made him turn.

She was sitting in the window seat, in the shadows.

"Drink?"

She shook her head.

"You look bad," he told her, fixing himself a drink. "Like something the cat dragged in. 'Cept it's Wills that got the cat treatment, isn't it?"

Cyndi still didn't answer.

"Cat got your tongue?" he asked. "Or did Point Harbor's finest wear you out with their relentless questioning?" Pretending to be concentrating on his drink, he watched her from beneath his eyelashes. He thought, but he wasn't sure, that she got even paler.

He smiled unpleasantly. "I'm surprised they let you go," he said. "Do they know how you tried to kill me once? Did you tell them that?"

Georgie woke up Monday morning with a bad headache. Bad dreams. She couldn't remember them, but they were definitely there.

The cops had not been nice to her. They'd treated her differently than they'd treated the others. But she'd made it clear she knew what was what. "I don't have to answer your questions," she'd told them. "Or am I under arrest? I know my rights."

They'd backed off a little at that. Then she'd told them what she knew — about Cyndi. And Wills. And the whole soap opera of the young and the richest. So that even if every one of those babes had lied and stuck together, someone was telling the truth.

Even if it wasn't the whole truth and nothing but.

That made her head stop hurting.

Her father's cat was meowing hungrily.

She hated that cat.

"Hungry?" she asked it.

The cat meowed.

"Thirsty?" she crooned.

The cat meowed.

"Tough, kitty, kitty," she called, and slammed the door behind her, laughing.

Cruising down Back Bay Road, Foy saw Dade slide out of Jones's car.

He almost stopped. But something about the whole setup made him keep going.

And start wondering.

Jones and Dade.

Definitely not situation normal.

What were they up to?

Then he told himself, stop it. You're getting paranoid. They're not up to anything.

They're probably just up. A little preschool meet to get high.

Except that it didn't fit. He'd never seen Dade carrying, much less getting high.

And Jones. Now there was a man who liked to stay in control.

Even that whole scene out at the Point, he'd been the ice of them all. The first one to reach Lara. To pull her away. Kneeling down beside the body and calmly checking for a pulse.

How had he even known where to look in all that — mess?

They said Wills had died instantly.

So everything else that had happened hadn't mattered.

But it mattered to the living. Someone out on the Point had done a Jack the Ripper on William Lawrence Howell.

Ironic.

Wills had always been such a fan of Jack's.

Foy turned into the parking lot.

Did he imagine it, or were the kids hanging nearby turning to stare? To whisper.

"Monday, Monday," muttered Foy, getting out of his car to face the day.

"Hey Foy, how'sit?" said one guy.

Brownie points to you, thought Foy.

Several more heads turned. Watching. Waiting.

Well, they weren't going to get anything from him.

"Hey," Foy said, and began to amble toward the school. He felt the eyes on him. Felt them watching.

He had the odd feeling that if he started to run, they'd all run after him, bring him down.

Then he thought about Halloween night out at the Point. How someone had been watching and waiting, then, too.

And, suddenly, although the day wasn't cold and he was wearing a jacket, he felt a chill down his neck.

It was cold as ice. As cold as death.

He felt fear ripping open his chest.

It took all his willpower not to turn. To make himself believe that nothing, *nothing* could possibly be behind him. That the killer, no way, could be standing out there in the parking lot, watching him.

At last he reached the doors of the school. Pulled them open.

But only when they slammed shut behind him did he feel safe.

Monday was going to be murder.

Chapter 8

"Part of our quaint charm," muttered Char.

She was in the Point Harbor public library, a carefully preserved pile of stones with narrow windows, drafty halls, and dark corners. She'd left school and come straight there to rummage in the stacks of crumbling, yellowing old newspapers that had not yet been converted to film.

Now, pulling a dusty bundle of newspapers off the lower shelf in the back of the stacks, she carried it to the rickety wooden table crammed in one corner of the basement. The corner was lit by an old lamp and the faint afternoon light of day coming through the small rectangular street-level windows at the top of the basement.

She was bored just being in the library. But what else was there to do? Homework? Not likely.

For a moment, she thought of Jones, and a little smile curved her lips. Not homework material. Exactly.

Then, resolutely putting him out of her mind, she blew the dust off the top of the stack and sneezed.

"*Gesundheit*," she said aloud.

She sat down and began to read.

Time passed.

Point Harbor history was hardly newsworthy, even when it had made the local newspaper. She'd started forty years back. That seemed far enough — unless whoever'd killed Wills was some kind of geriatric phenom.

Like Cyndi with a thousand face-lifts, she thought. Nah. I don't like Cyndi. But I don't think she's a killer, either.

Which still didn't explain what she was doing spending her downtime with a bunch of moldy old newspapers.

But maybe there was a pattern. Maybe someone like this had killed before.

"And maybe Jack the Ripper has been reincarnated in Point Harbor," she said sarcastically to herself.

Still, it helped to be busy. To think she might find something. It helped to keep her from thinking about, imagining, Wills's death. She hadn't liked Wills.

But no one deserved to die like that.

The light at the windows turned gray. She sifted through one stack of newspapers after another.

The police blotter reports gave new meaning to petty crime: a dispute over a fish stolen from the back of a truck. A rash of farm equipment thefts.

A local man charged with being a public nuisance for refusing to cut his lawn.

She even read the obituaries. But the deaths were natural. Car accidents, heart attacks, sad stories of illness and loss. Not murder.

Then, in the dead of winter in 1959, the murder-suicide of an old couple on their potato farm.

Expressions of shock on the part of the community.

Someone's car hit by a train.

A brief acknowledgment of the arrival of the Beatles.

And, late in the sixties, arrests for marijuana. One of the arrests had been of a farmer's daughter, growing marijuana in the cornfield.

Char made a disgusted sound and stood up and stretched. I don't spend this much time on homework, she thought. But, then, when was homework ever about murder?

Homework is murder, she thought.

She looked around at the shadowy stacks and thought, if you did your homework down here late enough, I suppose you could get murdered.

Ugh. But she wasn't really scared. The stacks were too depressing to be truly scary. She gathered up the last bundle of newspapers and trundled them to the back of the stacks.

Kneeling to shove the newspapers back in place on the lower shelf, she didn't hear anyone come in.

Instead, suddenly, she felt it — a shifting in the air. A flutter of the dim light.

She wasn't alone.

She straightened up slowly. Tried not to breathe.

The stacks were quiet. From upstairs, faintly, came the sound of the copier.

Nothing else.

Sure, she thought. Someone carrying a twelve-foot butcher knife and an ax and maybe a chain saw just oozed past the librarians on the way down here.

Sure.

Get a grip, Webster.

Besides, even if someone were down here, the librarians are just up the stairs. You wouldn't even have to scream very loud. And as long as you could scream . . .

She thought of Wills. Who hadn't made a sound.

She lifted her chin. Thought of her bare throat. Lowered her chin again. Took a deep breath. "Who's there?"

No one answered.

Her heart began to pound erratically.

"Stop that," she muttered.

And a soft, soft voice whispered in her ear, "Stop what?"

She didn't scream. Instead, grabbing a book from the nearest shelf, she spun around.

Jones said, "Wait."

"You!" Slowly, she lowered the book and pulled it close to her chest. She forced herself to speak. "Jones. What are you doing here?"

He held up a small black book. "I might ask the same thing."

Char recognized the artist's notebook she always carried with her. She'd left it on the table, where she had been taking notes and making sketches from the newspapers. "I might ask what you're doing with my property."

"Interesting stuff," he said, handing it to her casually.

"You had no right to look in that book."

"It was open," he said.

Had it been? She didn't think so. She wasn't sure. Taking the book, she pushed past him and headed back to the table where her leather shoulder satchel hung over the chair. Without looking at Jones, she shoved the book deep inside and hoisted the satchel.

"Hey, wait a minute," said Jones. Then, more softly, "I thought we were friends."

"Friends?" she echoed furiously. She kept remembering all the things she'd written in her notebook — not just notes from today, but personal things. Things she had never told anybody. She hoisted her satchel.

Jones blocked her way.

"I'm leaving now," she said pointedly.

"Char, hey, listen. I'm sorry. It was open. It really was. And I only looked at the open pages."

"You shouldn't have looked at anything."

"No, but I'm glad I did."

Startled, Char turned to face him. "What?"

Choosing his words carefully, Jones said, "We obviously think alike. We obviously pick up on some of the same things."

"We share vibes?" she said with soft sarcasm.

He ignored the sarcasm. "You're doing research on Wills's death, aren't you — looking up other crimes that happened around Point Harbor that might be similar."

"So?" He had her full attention now. Her thoughts took an unexpected spin back to Halloween night, the two of them in the car, right before Rick played his stupid joke.

"So," she repeated.

"The night Wills — died — you knew something was going to happen, too. You felt it."

"I don't know what I felt." She met Jones's eyes and added, "And whatever I felt, it didn't have anything to do with what happened."

They were the same height. Funny, she'd thought Jones was bigger, somehow. Taller.

He moved closer.

Involuntarily, she stepped back.

He stopped. "You don't trust me, do you?"

"Who killed Wills?" she returned. "Tell me that."

"I can't. I can't do that."

"You know," she said softly. "You do know."

They faced each other for a moment longer, both their faces in shadows. Her breath was coming in soft, short gasps. Whether it was rage, or fear, or some other emotion, or some combination of all, she couldn't tell.

Jones was breathing hard, too.

"The name," she said.

He didn't answer.

"Fine. Play the game," she said. "Keep the name. Excuse me. Please."

He stepped back to let her by.

When she reached the foot of the stairs, he said, "Char."

She stopped. She didn't turn around.

"It's not a game, Char."

"Then you won't mind if I don't play by the rules," she answered and went up the stairs.

Chapter 9

Georgina was bored.

Bored, bored, bored.

Bored to death.

The Halloween party had been ruined. Rotten party. And the weekend was still days away.

And Dorian hadn't called her, either. He'd said he would. Hadn't he? She was pretty sure he had. She'd had a little too much to drink, of course. She wasn't drunk. Never drunk. She could handle it. Quit any time.

But she didn't remember the whole evening all that clearly.

She hunched her shoulders and poured herself a little bit of vodka that she'd siphoned off the top of her father's supply. Fancy stuff he saved for special occasions. Made from potatoes.

It didn't matter. It all tasted the same. She took a sip and tried to think clearly now, her pale blue eyes squinting with the effort.

The cops had asked all kinds of questions. Had they believed her? What had Dorian told them? What had the others said about her?

She could just imagine. They always talked about her. Thought they were better than she was. Scared little girl Jane. That rich witch Cyndi. And Char. Charity. Ha. Ha to Lara, too. Looks weren't everything. You had to have brains, too.

What had happened to Wills was the least of what any one of them deserved. And weren't they scared now! Scared it was one of them. Trying to figure out who to blame.

Well they weren't going to blame her.

It served them all right.

Sorry. They'd all be sorry someday about how they'd treated her. When she was famous. Sorry.

But it was such a long time to wait. She wanted them to start being sorry sooner. Much sooner. Like now.

She finished her drink and picked up the phone.

"I don't think this is such a good idea." Dorian kept the BMW idling at the curb. A break-my-window, he called it. You can't park these in the city, he'd said. They break your window and take it all.

My next car is going to be a Jag, he'd said. This one will be the down payment.

She drove a two-door Toyota. When her father wasn't using it.

"Drive," she said now. "Or my old man'll come cracker-jackin' out the door, telling me it's a school night."

"Well, isn't it?" asked Dorian.

"Dorian."

"I'll drive. But Georgie-girl, my favorite brunette, what's the point?"

Why did he call her that junk name? Probably from one of those stupid old movies he was always watching. At first she'd thought they'd had something in common. But she couldn't stand the movies he liked. He was practically a freak.

But a rich freak.

"You have anything to drink?"

"Thanks, but I'm driving."

"Don't be stupid, Dorian."

"It's a school night for me, too."

"Yeah," she sneered. "You're on what? Halloween break from college? Why did you come home, Dorian?"

"You called and made me an offer I couldn't refuse," he said lightly, but she could see it annoyed him. Good. She liked him a little annoyed. A little upset.

She said, "I'm flattered you decided to stay on. Or maybe the cops asked you to."

"Or maybe they didn't." Dorian turned the car into a convenience store parking lot and got out. A few minutes later he returned with a six-pack in a brown bag.

"For me? How sweet."

He didn't answer as he started up the car. Then he said shortly, "Keep it down, okay. I don't want my license pulled for having an open beer in the car with a minor attached to it."

"You don't mind having a minor in your car doing other things," she said.

"Dif, Georgie. Big time."

"Bogus, Dorian. It's just as illegal. Isn't it?"

They were out of town now, negotiating the narrow turns along the Back Bay Road. The houses along Back Bay weren't as impressive as the ones on the beach. But those houses, sitting deep in their nest of woods with their walks to private bay beaches and their waterviews, they cost enough, thought Georgie.

"Why are we doing this?" asked Dorian.

Because I'm bored, thought Georgie. Because I like a little thrill, and you aren't cutting it.

Aloud she said, "You remember Nancy Drew, girl detective? Or how 'bout Sherlock? Well, I thought it might be fun to look for some clues. You know?"

"I don't know," answered Dorian impatiently. "It's a mega-ditz idea, Georgie. The whole Point is sealed off, for one thing. And it's almost dark, for another."

"It won't be dark for at least another hour," she said scornfully. "What'sa matter. Scared?"

His lips tightened. "No."

"They think Cyndi did it," she said, just to see his lips tighten a little more.

He didn't answer, so Georgina went on. "She's capable of it, don't you think? I mean, she's got such a bad temper. And she's strong. A big strong . . ."

"What about it?"

"Why do you always get so bent over Cyndi?" asked Georgie. "What's with you and her?"

"We're going back to the scene of the crime, Georgie. We're going to look for clues, as you so professionally described it. You're going to get to be Nancy Drew for an hour. So just be quiet."

Georgie leaned back, satisfied. For the moment. "Nice sunset," she said.

Dorian didn't answer.

The gate to Cemetery Point was padlocked shut. The "No Trespassing — Danger" sign was back up. Neon police tape sealed the scene of the crime.

"What now?" said Dorian.

"Can you walk?" asked Georgie.

Without waiting for an answer, she slid out of the car and headed toward the gate. "C'mon," she said. "Help me."

She slithered through as Dorian reluctantly held the strands of barbed wire apart. He followed, being careful not to snag his lambskin jacket.

"Start looking for clues," she said, taking a long swallow of beer.

"For clues. Yeah, sure. If I see any suspicious trees, I'll run right over and make a citizen's arrest."

They walked in silence down the sandy, rutted path.

"Oh, wow," said Dorian sarcastically. "Something big's been here. Look at those tracks. And the broken branches. Maybe a car?"

"Oh, Sherlock, you really turn me on," Georgie snapped back.

The silence descended again. So very quiet. Dorian couldn't quite put his finger on it. . . . "Doesn't this give you the creeps?" he asked.

"No," said Georgie. "It's exciting."

In the clearing by the graveyard, they stopped by the charred remains of the fire. "The cooler's gone," he noted. "Guess the cops took it."

He started to kick ashes and rubble, then thought about all the television shows he'd seen about preserving the evidence, and stopped.

"Wills brought it back this way." Georgie caught his hand.

Her hand was very warm. Hot. She squeezed his fingers and smiled brilliantly back at him.

Tough cookie, Georgie. With *a lot* of weird energy. But exciting. Something about her excitement now, the way she was obviously getting off on this whole sick scene, was turning him on, too, now.

Sick.

"It's getting dark," he said.

"You are *such* a chicken." She turned to face him, her eyes shining. "Come *on*."

Dorian tugged her toward him. "What's in it for me?"

"What d'ya want to be in it?" She pulled back, keeping just out of reach of his other arm, her smile bright. "Come with me, and I'll show you."

"What a bad little girl you are," he said, following. "You're really getting off on this, aren't you?"

"Aren't you?" she asked. "Nothing ever happens. Now something has. Doesn't that do anything for you?"

"Murder doesn't."

"Danger, then."

He started to point out that there wasn't any danger. Whoever'd done Wills was long gone. The only danger was someone finding out.

Instead, he allowed himself to be led along, trying to step in the footprints Georgie made. If anyone found out about this, he didn't want his footprints all over the place. Although, come to think of it, he could have made those footprints on Halloween.

Suddenly Georgie stopped with a little gasp. Her fingers tightened on his.

The chalk outline where Wills's body had been glowed eerily in the early dusk. More darkly, great stains grouted the cracked earth and seared grass inside and around the outline.

Blood.

All of the blood in Wills's body, from the look of it.

"Wow," breathed Georgie. She strained forward, gazing avidly.

"Careful," he said. She seemed not to have heard him as she dropped his hand and walked closer.

"Look, Dorian. This is where Wills fell. Backwards. And Lara must have knelt down here. That means whoever stabbed him, stabbed him from the front."

"That doesn't necessarily mean you fall backwards," said Dorian.

"Then maybe he was tripped. Or dragged."

In spite of himself, the whole grisly scene was getting to him. He said, softly, "Do you see any drag marks, Georgie? Look, we don't know enough to find any clues. And whatever clues there were, the police found them."

Georgie remained a moment longer, kneeling where Lara had knelt. She was imagining herself as a great actor. The cameras were all on her. She'd handle it better than Lara. . . .

"Georgie."

"Oh, all right!" She got up crossly and brushed the dirt off her jeans. "We're going, we're going." She looked up at him. "Kiss?"

When he looked up again, it was almost dark.

"We gotta go."

Georgie pressed against him. "Now?"

For an answer, he pulled her against him and started toward the graveyard entrance.

"Wait," said Georgie. She reached down, picked up her beer, and finished it. Then she threw the bottle as far as she could.

"Why don't you just leave a note saying you were here," said Dorian.

"I dropped it that night. When we were playing hide-and-seek. You're the only one who knows different." She smiled suddenly. "Let's go, Dorian. Let's go have some *fun*."

He didn't want to admit how relieved he was. Instead, he said, "Tell me about it." If they walked quickly, they'd be out of there before it got too dark.

He was wrong. The darkness in the woods was already complete. He picked up his pace.

"Hey," Georgie complained. "I've got on boots with heels, okay?"

"Come *on*." He hurried ahead. An uneasy feeling was growing on him. The branches of the trees felt disquietingly like hands, holding on to him. And the silence.

That silence. No birds. No animals rustling in the undergrowth. No squirrels or gulls. *Nada*.

Nothing. Complete silence.

Like the grave.

"You're scared, aren't you?" Georgie's voice took on a mocking note. "You're really scared."

"Will you come on?" They were in the clearing. He was almost running now.

"What a cowardly little boy." He reached the head of the rutted sand track leading back to the gate. Looked back.

Georgie had stopped dead and was standing there, her arms folded, one hip thrust out provocatively, her black hair like a dark halo around her head. While he watched, she ran her tongue over her lips, then caught the lower one in her teeth. Her eyes were bright, supernaturally bright.

"Don't you want to stay for a while, little boy?"

She unfolded her arms, and ran one hand down her hip.

For a moment, he almost turned around.

Then he heard it. The faintest of sounds in the undergrowth.

"Hurry," he said.

He crashed forward, pushed his way toward the gate. The last sliver of sun snuffed out below the horizon.

"Dorian!" Georgie's voice, suddenly sharp. Looking over his shoulder, he saw her behind him.

"Run," he ordered. He didn't stop.

The barbed wire tore at his hands. At his jacket. He didn't care.

He didn't care about the torn leather, the torn flesh on his palms and fingers.

For a moment it felt as if the wire were holding on to him. He gave a strangled cry and tore free.

Crouching, sobbing, he reached the car. The blood on his hands made the door handle slippery.

"C'mon, come on," he sobbed.

Then he was inside. He slammed the door shut behind him.

Georgie's window was down. Frantically he fumbled for the button to roll it up.

It wouldn't work.

Power windows.

Break my window.

He jammed the key into "on." The engine screamed.

The window began to grind shut.

"Dorian!" He saw her just beyond the gate in the trees.

"Dorian!" she screamed. It was a voice he'd never heard before.

"Come on, dammit!" At the same time, almost involuntarily, his fingers found the automatic lock.

All four doors locked with a clunk.

"Runnnn!" he screamed.

But Georgie wasn't running. She wasn't hurrying at all. It was almost as if she were moving in slow motion. In slow motion, she turned her head. In slow motion, she stumbled.

"Dor . . ."

Something dark leapt out of the woods.

He shifted into gear.

There was a glint of burning metal light.

Georgie turned back to face it. Whirled in a grotesque dance. And then jumped, as if she were rising up to meet the glittering blade.

The car bucked wildly in the soft earth. For one awful moment, he thought it was going to stall.

He didn't see Georgie fall.

He tore down the track, heedless of the branches scoring the side of the car.

Heedless of what had fastened to the door handle.

Chapter 10

Cyndi was driving. She'd started out driving aimlessly. Then she had started tailing people, trying to guess where they were going by their cars, then following them to see how close she came.

The Mercedes had stopped at the grocery store. Not even close.

The farm truck had pulled around behind Finisterre, the pricey hotel overlooking the bay.

She'd missed that one, too. Some detective.

A police car cruised by. Was she being followed?

So far, there had been no more questions from the cops. It was one of the advantages of having rich parents and a nasty lawyer in a nice suit.

But that didn't mean she wasn't being followed.

She edged out of town. Maybe if she laid down some fast miles, she'd feel better.

And if someone *was* following her, let them try and keep up.

After all, a suspected murderer wouldn't mind playing a little chicken.

"I'm home," called Char.

At almost the same instant, a herd of snorting, stamping, mooing children shot by, pursued by her stepfather and one of her sisters riding on her stepfather's shoulders.

"Giddyap, bang, bang, bang!" screamed her sister.

"I don't think you're supposed to shoot the cows," said Char wryly.

Her stepfather rolled his eyes.

"Bang, bang, bang!" shrieked her sister, pointing at Char. "You're dead, too."

"Not quite," said Char. She went back to her room and shut the door.

Slinging the satchel on the desk, she reached inside for her notebook. She found it . . . and another book.

A pale rusty-colored book, the rust of black cloth faded with age. Nothing was written on the outside. Inside, the printing was close and faded to an even paler rust. Almost indecipherable.

Almost.

"Where did this come from?" she muttered. She fluttered the pages. The book smelled old, as if the pages had not been turned in a long, long time.

Had it fallen into her pack at the library? She tried to remember if she'd seen any other old books like this.

And then Char felt the hair rise on her neck. In her own house, in her own room, and she was spooked. Worse than the time she'd read that book, what was it — *Interview with the Vampire*.

Only this wasn't an interview, and this wasn't fiction. It was an old whaler's journal. Something printed before the turn of the century.

And across the title page, in the same faded rusty script, was the title: *Of Darkness and Its Minions*.

"No," she said aloud. And in spite of herself, began to read.

What am I doing here? thought Cyndi. Who do I think I am, Florence Nightingale?

More like Dr. Strangelove. Or something.

She rang the front doorbell.

A few minutes later she was standing just inside the door of Lara's bedroom.

"Lara?"

Lara was sitting in a chair by the window. The curtains were almost drawn shut, and the room was in near darkness.

"Lara?"

Without turning her head, Lara said in a flat, lifeless voice, "What."

"It's me. Cyndi. Remember me?"

"I'm fine," said Lara. "Thanks for stopping by."

"And I can go now? C'mon, Lara."

Slowly, at last, Lara turned to look at Cyndi. It was hard to see her expression in the dim room. The silence between them lengthened.

97

"Knock it off, Lara," Cyndi said abruptly, and sat down on the bed and folded her legs beneath her. "What's going on here?"

That made Lara sit up. "Wills is dead. I was *there*."

"So was I. And I wasn't any more in love with him than you are — were."

"There's blood all over my dress. Blood all over me. . . ."

"Get a new dress. Take a bath."

"Oh! You are hateful. A real piece of . . ."

"I am, but what's that got to do with it? C'mon, Lara. This is the kind of thing Georgie would do — Melodrama 101."

The hiss of Lara's breath told Cyndi she'd scored. She waited.

Then Lara said, "Why are you here?"

"Why are you? Gonna hide out until it's all over?"

Then Lara said, in a smaller, different voice, "Yes."

Cyndi leaned forward. "Why?"

"Because," said Lara.

"Lara."

"Because," repeated Lara. "Because . . . I saw who killed Wills. And I don't want him to kill me."

Ghost ships. Monster sharks.

Superstition and blood. And death.

A history of it. One that came at last around to Point Harbor.

Only it wasn't Point Harbor then. It was Cemetery Point.

"... Because there be besides a graveyard on that tongue or spitt of land that enfoldeth the harbor, just beyond as grave a stretch of treachery water, marked by ungodly tyde and hidden rock, as ever known to man, and beying called the Devil's Teeth."

Not big news. All other things being equal, she was surprised they hadn't made old Cemetery Point into a sort of amusement park, with quarter-operated telescopes for a closer look at the Devil's Teeth.

But there was more. The sudden closing of Cemetery Point, alluded to only as a done deal in the local newspaper she'd read earlier in the library, was foreshadowed here in the unidentified author's words.

No one went to Cemetery Point now, the author noted, to bury their dead. They chose the newer graveyard inland. For though it was true that those sailors who were not "gatheryed into the bosom of the waves" might prefer a burial within sight of the sea, it was also true that "upon that once hallowed land there now be hauntings.

"For it is the port of call of one fiend ship, that doth sail easily among the rocks and across the tydes, doth land where no ship can land, doth lure other mortal ships to immortal death, that it might gathyr souls from proper burial. That evidence be those who search the shore after a ship goeth down, they find no bodyes whole, but such rendered parts as was done by no earthly element.

"Some do saye that the master of the fiend ship be a foul dark creature, huge and graven, escap'd from Englund by reason of unspeakable renderings of human flesh therein that country, and thus driven forth to come hence here to our sorrow, having devoured his crew in feasts of blood."

"Sharks," she whispered. "It was sharks." She read on:

"Some do say that Thing which waityth upon the Cemetery Point and beyond, cannot be destroyed. That it hath Powers: to fly, to mimick form and life and shadow, to come and go, to suck upon the heart all that is hiddyn there. That it can only be stopped before it grow yet stronger still. But none have come upon the means to stop it, not one yet having seeing its face and lived."

Char swallowed, her mouth dry. "Impossible," she whispered.

Then, much later, a final entry, the handwriting

suddenly shrunken, as if written by a shaken, aging hand:

"I have seen Her there. She hath died outside Godliness for she movves yet upon the land and water. Howsomever, I do not belieyve she did mayke tryst and pact with the Dark. What was buried was not buried arright. The Peace is made of wronged blood.

"She was beautiful once."

The journal ended abruptly. There was no more.

It's not possible, Char repeated to herself. What had happened is someone had found this account, or one like it, and had used it to stage Wills's murder.

But if someone had it, and had used it as a handbook for murder, what was it doing in her pack? How had it gotten there?

Then she remembered Jones, standing there in the shadows in the basement in the library.

And it suddenly made vampires seem easy.

Chapter 11

I handled that all wrong, thought Cyndi.

I've got to be careful. Or people really will think I did it.

Because Lara had suddenly gone still. And silent. "Go away," was all she would say. "Go away."

And I made a fool of myself, thought Cyndi. I actually begged Lara to help me.

Cyndi flushed, remembering her words. "For me, Lara," she'd said. "We're friends."

"Friends?" Lara had answered slowly, in a considering voice.

And nothing more.

Maybe she won't remember that I begged, Cyndi thought. Maybe she's too scared.

But who had Lara seen?

What had she seen?

Maybe they'll believe Lara did it, Cyndi thought. After all, she had all that blood on her dress. What if she didn't get it kneeling down beside the body?

Maybe that's *why* she threw herself down by

Wills. To explain why she already had blood on her dress.

What normal person would throw themselves down by a hacked-up corpse?

Then she thought, Lara? A hatchet woman? Cyndi, get real.

The car purred along. No one knew where she was. Not that anyone cared. The parental units were out partying for charity at some big-bucks-a plate dinner. Her brother was holed up in his room.

Her brother. As always, the thought of Dorian made her feel crazy. What a sick puppy he was. She hadn't liked him from the moment she was born.

But, then, he hadn't liked her, either.

Still, after what had happened, you wouldn't think he'd have the nerve to go on scorching her.

Scorching. Funny she should choose that word.

Where was Dorian? Strange big bro Dorian. Now *he* was someone who was capable of murder.

A little smile curved her lips. Yes. Dorian. Maybe Dorian did it.

When she got home, it was late. But she wasn't tired. In fact, she was high. Manically high. The energy poured through her, bright, unstoppable.

Her parents' Continental was still out. So was Dorian's BMW. She slotted her car into its space, powered the garage door closed behind her. She'd just gotten out of her car when she heard the sound.

Dorian's car.

She stepped back in the shadows and waited as the garage door went back up.

He was driving like a bat out of hell.

He slammed the car into the last space at the far end of the garage, fendering the wall at the end and bouncing back. He slammed the door open so hard, it rebounded against the wall.

That, thought Cyndi, is going to make a nice dent.

He staggered around the front of the car, his breath coming in rasps.

Cyndi smiled a little.

She stepped forward from the shadows.

"Hot date?" she asked nastily.

And her big, brave brother screamed.

The lights of the patrol car swept the gate. The cop behind the wheel frowned. Something wasn't right.

She swore softly and began to report back on the radio. The other cop got out, one hand on his gun, and played this flashlight over the scene.

"Ten-four," she said. She slid out of the car and flicked on her own flashlight. The shadows jumped in the crisscrossing beams of light. The gate made long bars of darkness on the other side.

"Can you see anything?" she asked.

"I'm not sure."

Leaving the car lights on and the motor running, they cautiously approached the gate.

"Look," she said.

Something torn fluttered on the barbed wire. They bent down to examine it.

"Leather," she said at last. "A strip of leather. A shoe?"

"A jacket," suggested her partner.

"Yeah . . . it wasn't here before. . . ."

She shone her bright light through the wire, back into the shadows, quartering the darkness.

The silent eerie darkness.

"You watching my back?" she asked.

Any other time, he might have made some pig joke. And she would have called him a pig. Laughed. Or given him grief, depending.

But, tonight, he just said, "Yeah."

"There are two of us, anyway," she went on.

"There were ten of them," he answered. "To begin with."

"Who would be stupid enough to come out here after something like that?"

"Thrill-seekers. Ghouls."

It was her turn to answer, "Yeah."

She turned her flashlight to a new section of darkness. Swept it again. Froze.

Something lay motionless in the white beam.

Something horrible.

Something that had once been human.

For one moment, she wanted to say, "Call the cops."

Then she remembered: *I am one.*

Whatever — whoever — it had been, it was still oozing.

Maybe whoever it was, was still alive.

Sort of.

"Oh, my god," said her partner behind her.

Cyndi walked across the garage. She'd never seen Dorian so scared.

Or almost never, anyway.

He'd bolted out of the garage like the devil himself was following.

She was smiling, a little. Funny how, if you did something and someone blamed you for it, it made you hate them worse than ever.

The way she hated her dear, sweet brother.

Then she stopped, the smile leaving her lips.

Her heart began to pound heavily.

"Dorian?" she whispered. She walked forward again, stopping by the driver's side of the door.

Dorian had a lot more to worry about than a little dent in his car door.

The words of Rick's stupid, tired old Halloween tale came back to her.

Only it didn't seem like such a stupid story anymore, did it?

Because a deep gouge ran down one side of the car. And hanging on the handle on the driver's side was a bloody hook.

"Dorian."

No answer.

"Dorian. I know you're in there."

A long pause. Then he said, "Why don't you just

go away, Cyndi. Don't you think you've done enough?"

She tried the handle of the door. It was locked. She jiggled it impatiently.

"I think we need to have a little talk."

He didn't answer.

"I think we need to talk about what happened . . . tonight."

No answer. But a minute later, the doorknob turned in her hand.

He didn't open it for her. "It's unlocked," he said and had already started retreating to the other side of the room when she pushed her way in.

He turned to face her from the corner. Like an animal, his back against the wall.

"What do you want, Cyndi?"

"What happened tonight?"

His face, if possible, got paler. "Nothing."

"Nothing?" She raised her brows. "Nothing?"

He remained silent. Watching. Waiting.

"Where did you go, Dorian?"

"Out."

"Who'd you go with?"

"Nobody."

"And you didn't do nothing," she mocked him.

"I drove around," he said.

"Well, you must have hit something." She paused, watching him watch her.

He made a sound. A strangled sound.

She was enjoying this. She was. She said, softly,

persuasively, "Remember, Dorian? Remember when I was five, and you were seven?"

That sound again. But now color was coming back into his face. Color and rage.

"Remember how you used to play hide-and-seek with me, Dorian? And how you locked me in the trunk in the attic? And how you were going to leave me there?"

"You're lying."

"Nooo. No. It's the truth. Only you wimped. *After* I'd been there for hours. Alone. Buried alive. In the dark."

The strangled sound again.

Her voice grew soft. "You'd think I'd be afraid of the dark, after that, wouldn't you, Dorian? A scared little kid. A coward. But it didn't work out that way."

"I came back for you," he whispered. "It was a joke."

"No, it didn't work out the way you planned. Because what doesn't kill you makes you stronger."

"It was a joke." He licked his lips. "A joke."

She smiled. "I'm laughing. See?"

He rasped out, "What you tried was murder."

"But you *made* me keep playing hide-and-seek. That stupid game. Why did you? So you could try to scare me to death again? Or so you could really kill me?"

"You're crazy!"

"I don't think so. Then I was. A crazy little kid,

to keep playing a crazy little game with her crazy big brother."

She paused. Smiled. "But not now."

"It wasn't me. Not . . . it wasn't me who tried to do the killing," he said raggedly.

"Oh, Dorian. What *are* you saying? I locked you in that closet because I was afraid of you. Then. Did you think I would do to you what you did to me? That I wouldn't let you out?"

"The fire," he said.

"An accident, Dorian."

"It was the fire department that let me out!"

She said softly, "I told them you were there. I told them. I told them. I saved your life. You should thank me."

"Get out," he said.

"And I've been the one they've blamed ever since. Not you. Me."

"Get out!"

"I'm going," she said. "But if I were you, I wouldn't let anybody else drive my car."

Chapter 12

"I don't like you, Dade," said Jane.

Dade leaned out of the car window, one hand draped over the steering wheel, the other resting on the car door.

"If you don't like me, why are you talking to me?"

Jane shook her head and kept walking.

"You shouldn't be out so late alone," offered Dade.

"And you should?" she shot back.

"I'm with you."

She spun to face him. "You are not! Can't you just leave me alone!"

He twisted the car up onto the grassy verge just in front of her and stopped. With one quick, easy motion he jumped out and stood facing her.

She stepped back. It was hard to read his expression in the dark.

"What do you want?" she asked, keeping her voice cold.

"I'll walk with you," he said. "Unless you want me to give you a ride."

She hesitated. Which was worse — walking alongside Dade? Or riding in the car with him — alone?

She was so tired. So afraid. So alone. The cops had been back. Everyone at school kept watching. Waiting. Foy was acting weird. Like he wasn't all there. And Char wasn't even home. Where was she?

What was going on?

Murder, she thought. Murder is what's going on.

No one was acting normal.

She didn't have anyone to talk to. So she'd come for a walk. Just a short walk in her very well-tended, carefully guarded neighborhood.

The hedges were way too thick for anyone to hide in. The private security force had already swung by once. She'd waved, and they'd recognized her.

Safe. Probably safer to walk than to get in the car with Dade.

So why, then, did she suddenly want to live dangerously?

"Does Cyndi know where you are?" she asked.

His teeth flashed white in the dark. "And I don't know where she is, either."

"Let's go for a ride," she said recklessly.

He held open the driver's door with a little bow, and she got in and slid across to the passenger seat.

She'd never been in Dade's car alone before. It

felt bigger. The motor sounded like one of those cars her father used to drive.

Her father. She missed him. But missing wouldn't bring back the dead.

They pulled away from the curb. Drove down the manicured lanes between the hedges.

"Where do you want to go?" asked Dade.

"Far, far away," she answered without thinking.

"Oz?" he said.

"Not exactly," she answered slowly. "But somewhere that isn't here."

"No place that isn't," he said. "Every place turns into here sooner or later."

She thought about that. Shook her head. "Wherever I go, it's going to be different. I'm going to be different."

"Changing the props don't change the performer," said Dade.

"Maybe I just don't want to perform anymore," she snapped.

He turned to look at her quickly. Grinned. "Good," he said.

"You're strange, Dade," she said. She couldn't believe she was sitting here, talking to him like that.

"Wait'll you get to know me," he said.

She slid a little closer. This isn't me, she thought. Does Cyndi act like this all the time? Is this what it feels like for Georgie when she's after someone? Or Lara?

"I don't want to wait," she said. *Oh, my god, I can't believe I said that. It's like I'm possessed.*

But Dade didn't seem to mind. He pulled the car to a stop.

Jane looked out. They were on the beach, above the dunes, opposite Cemetery Point.

She had a brief moment to think about Halloween and Cemetery Point and Wills.

A briefer moment to think about Cyndi.

Then she stopped thinking altogether.

Dorian's face was ugly. His hands were shaking.

In the harsh overhead light of the garage, he was staring at the door of his car. At the bloody gouge scored down one side.

At the bloody hook hanging on the door.

Someone is trying to scare me, he thought. It was an oddly comforting thought.

Because if someone wasn't, if this wasn't some sick, elaborate joke . . .

But it had to be. Georgie probably wasn't even dead. This whole Captain Hook routine was . . . was . . . yes, probably Cyndi's idea.

Or it was a frame-up?

No.

No one would believe it.

He wasn't thinking clearly. He had to stop panicking.

He took a deep breath. Time to ease on down the road, he thought.

Like now.

But where?

He couldn't go back to school. Being suspended

for cheating had put that away for him.

Money, I've got plenty of money, he thought. I'll think of something.

The important thing was to get away.

He turned.

He almost screamed.

Someone was standing in the corner of the garage. She walked toward him. He raised shaking hands, as if to ward her off.

Then he realized he was right. It had all been some awful joke. His worst fears weren't coming true.

Georgie wasn't really dead.

"Sick," he said. "You're sick, Georgie. Did that turn you on, doing that to me? You got so hot off it, you had to come and find me? That it?"

Georgie stopped.

She tilted her head. "Is that what you think?" she asked.

Dorian started toward her, his hands clenched.

Georgie waited. Smiling.

"Jane," Dade said softly.

Jane laughed. Phooey on Foy, she thought. Why didn't someone tell me the truth?

She sensed, rather than saw Dade smile.

"Having fun?" she whispered.

"Umm."

"I am. So far."

He shifted a little, holding her. She felt his breath in her hair.

They stayed that way for a while. Still. Which wasn't bad, either.

Then she turned toward him. Pulled him against her hard.

His arms tightened for just a moment.

Then he said sharply, "I don't believe this."

That made her remember who she was. And what she was doing.

She tried to twist free, but his arms tightened even more.

"Dade," she gasped.

"I don't believe this," he repeated.

And then she saw it. Saw the flashing lights out on Cemetery Point. Saw them careening away toward town along the coast road.

Dade let her go abruptly. As Jane caught her breath, he kicked the car into gear.

A moment later they were speeding back toward Point Harbor.

"It's happening again, isn't it?" she said, almost to herself, as they roared through the night.

And then she thought, I wonder which one of us it is this time.

The nice thing about the BurgerBurger was that they didn't care how long you stayed, as long as it wasn't crowded, thought Char. She'd been there for a couple of hours. It was comforting, the jelly bean colors, the relentless piped-in music. It had driven her crazy when she'd worked there, but now she liked it.

She watched the sophomore behind the counter, an intense kid with sandy hair and a collection of earrings in one ear. She was flirting, carefully, with a couple of guys who were sitting at the table closest to the counter.

Char would have told her from long experience that no matter how carefully she flirted, the manager knew. It was like she had eyes in the back of her head.

But she'd let it ride as long as the counter help didn't take it too far. Or give away too many free fries.

I should go over to Jane's, thought Char. But she didn't want to. She just wanted to sit there. Peacefully. Safely.

She wanted to sit here and not think about Jones. Or love. Or death. Funny how those three things seemed to go together.

About as funny as her dreams.

She slid her hand into her pack and touched the spine of the journal. Next to it was a fat paperback full of explanations of dreams and their symbols that she'd found on her mother's shelf. Her mother said books like that helped her understand what the art critics were talking about.

It hadn't helped Char.

Because it wasn't a dream, thought Char. *It was real.*

Suddenly the BurgerBurger felt confining. She needed to move. She needed to think.

No! She needed to stop thinking.

She gave herself a mental shake and looked at her watch. It *was* getting sort of late. Time to cruise.

Char walked slowly across the parking lot of the BurgerBurger. I smell like McGrease, she thought wryly. But she'd needed the comfort food. Funny, when she'd worked there, she'd sworn she'd never eat another burger. But, now, sometimes, it was just what she wanted.

Her pack bumped against her. She felt the edge of the book.

She took a long, comforting slurp of mocha shake.

Then she heard it. No, sensed it.

Someone was behind her.

But that was crazy. Of course someone was behind her. This was the Point Harbor town parking lot. The BurgerBurger was doing a brisk business. And some of the other stores, the ones that were still open, had just started to close for the night. People were coming out of them now, headed toward their cars.

Car doors slammed. Motors idled. People talked and waved.

She looked behind her, anyway.

No one.

She hurried more quickly to her car and fumbled with the key. Why wouldn't the door open?

There. Now. A quick check of the back seat, and then . . .

The blinding glare of headlights pinned her against the darkness.

Even though she'd never seen Georgie's father, she knew that was who was standing at the Emergency Room door. For one thing, they looked alike.

For another, Jane recognized the battered two-door Toyota next to him, the driver's door still open. A police officer was saying something to him, her face a frozen mask of professional sympathy. But he didn't seem to be listening.

Dade pulled into the parking lot and led the way toward the ER entrance.

It was a small hospital. A small hospital in a quiet town. It wasn't accustomed to handling anything like this. But, still, the professionals had stepped into their roles, bustling, rapping out orders as a stretcher was lowered gingerly from the ambulance and hustled through the ER doors. Beyond, the scene was one of frantic motion and scalding white light. But the bundle lay motionless and silent.

It was done with all the noise.

Jane swallowed hard and looked quickly down at her fists.

"What happened?" Dade asked the driver of the ambulance.

The driver shook his head. "Nobody knows. But it looks like she really bought it. Like that other guy out there. Looks like she got a dose of Jack the Ripper."

"Georgina," said Jane softly. "It was Georgina."

"They dunno yet," said the driver. "Hey, you shouldn't be here."

He got back in the ambulance and began to back it away from the ER door.

Georgina's father had gone inside. They could see him, two more cops with him now.

Just then a tall man with streaks of silver in his short, tightly curled black hair came toward them. He was in a white coat and had a stethoscope around his neck. He took off his glasses. Rubbed his nose.

For a moment, it seemed as if all the movement had stopped.

Just like a play, thought Jane wonderingly.

Then the doctor slowly shook his head.

And Jane knew Georgina was dead, too.

"Rick! Foy! You guys scared me! Don't you know how to honk or something?" Char was really annoyed, more at herself than anything.

"Yo, Charity," said Rick.

"What d'you want, Rick?" she asked.

"Nothing. We were just hanging and saw you and . . ." he shrugged.

"Well, nice seeing you and all, but I've got to get home."

Foy said, "We were kind of looking for Jane."

Char frowned.

"I called. She wasn't home. She was out for a walk," Foy explained.

"Well, she didn't walk this far." Char was still frowning. She knew Jane liked to take walks sometimes. But this wasn't exactly the safest time to do it.

Rick said, "So she's probably back home by now, my man."

But Foy looked as unconvinced as Char felt. Fishing in her pockets, Char brought up some change. She nodded toward the phone booth at the corner of the parking lot. "I'm going to go give her a quick call, okay?"

"Good idea," said Foy. "We'll wait."

But when Char reached Jane's house, Jane wasn't back yet.

"I'll tell Miss Jane you called," Hodges said firmly when Char tried to ask more questions.

And Char suddenly began to feel very, very afraid.

"Georgie? Georgina?"

She took a step toward him this time.

He took a step back.

"You're not really dead," he insisted. His voice was a croak. He could feel the sweat on the palms of his hands. Feel it starting up on his forehead. Funny you could be so sweaty and so cold at the same time.

"Oh, I'm not dead," Georgie agreed sweetly. "I'm very, very hard to kill." She took another step toward him.

He took another step back. Felt the cool metal of his car beneath his hands.

Smelled the rank smell of sweat. And another

smell. A cloying stench. A dead smell.

"Georgie," he whispered.

And now another, sharper smell. Gasoline.

"Get away," he said hoarsely. "Don't come any closer."

The sweat ran into his eyes. He blinked, brought his arm up and dragged it across them.

The figure blurred.

"Who are you?" he asked. He could barely breathe. Darkness swam at the edge of his senses.

The figure smiled. "Who do you want me to be?" it asked coquettishly. It reached down, came up with a pack of cigarettes and a match. It took a cigarette out of the pack.

"You killed Wills, didn't you?" gasped Dorian. "And . . . and Georgie."

It smiled, the unlit cigarette clenched between its teeth.

"Who shall I be?" it asked. "The first time, I was a sorry sight. I could barely get it together to give Wills, what he . . . wanted. But, then, with sweet Georgina, I could be a little more creative."

"Jack the Ripper?" Dorian could feel the cold to his bones. Could feel how the horrible cold was making his bones crumble inside him.

He was shaking.

"Cold, Dorian?" The figure flipped open a book of matches. "Jack the Ripper. Hmm. Or Clarence. Or in the nautical line, Captain. Or Charon. But I like Jack. A very high profile image. Yes. Jack will do for now."

The figure struck the match. Made an elaborate show of lighting the cigarette. "Care for a light?" it asked.

Dorian felt himself losing consciousness.

"Get away . . . get away," Dorian gasped. He felt himself sliding into unconsciousness.

The lit match flew through the air.

And the world exploded into flame and darkness.

"Yes," it said. "Yes. Tell them — Jack's back."

Chapter 13

Char was halfway back across the parking lot when she heard the explosion. For a moment, she didn't believe it was real. For a moment, she thought it was her senses, playing that trick on her. Making bogus earthquakes.

Then she heard the fire station's siren down the street go into action, calling all the volunteers.

"Hot, hot, hot," cracked Rick as she reached her car.

"Jane's still not home," Char told Foy. "I — "

"Let's go see the fire," interrupted Rick.

"You are so cold!" She felt her temper flare up. "Don't you care that something might have happened to Jane?"

"Maybe it's her house that's on fire," said Rick. "It's in the right direction."

Controlling her disgust — barely — Char swung around. It *was* the right direction.

"It's not Jane's house," Foy said, but he was getting back into his car.

"Yeah, maybe it's your house," said Rick.

"Give me a break," Foy said.

"Grow up," muttered Char. She wheeled and raced back toward her Mom's old Volvo. Miraculously, it started on the first try.

She could hear the sirens of the fire truck as it pulled away from the station. Ahead of her, Foy and Rick were turning out of the parking lot. Too slow. Too slow.

She put her hand on the horn. "Go, go for God's sake, move it!" she screamed.

The hospital had disappeared into the night behind them.

They were tracing their way through the dark, following the flickering light.

The light of a fire.

Whatever it is, thought Jane, it can't be any worse. "Turn here," she said aloud.

And then she realized who lived at the end of that street, and she knew Dade realized it, too.

And realized that, yes, it could be worse. Much, much worse.

A fire in Point Harbor was a big event. But a fire in the rich section of town was ranked public entertainment. The public was already there, pulling up in its cars, leaning out of windows, standing on roofs to see the show.

Ahead of her, Dade pushed his way unceremoniously through the gathering crowd. A few muttered complaints. But no one tried to interfere with him.

A fire fighter stopped them at the edge of the tangle of hoses.

"It's the garage, Dade," Jane said. "Just the garage."

But just the garage was enough, burning like the fires from some Bible-thumper's sermon, lighting up the sky. The fire fighters worked frantically, trying to contain it, trying to keep it from spreading.

"What happened?" Jane asked the beefy guy next to her.

"Like, an explosion," said the beefy guy. He burped. He was holding a beer, and his pot belly threatened to pop the zipper on his jacket.

A murmur went up from the crowd as the front door of the house opened and a figure in a uniform tottered out escorted by a fire fighter. She joined two other figures at the edge of the lawn.

"Is that everybody?" shouted the chief.

Jane knew the answer before the fire fighter could start shaking his head.

"No!" he shouted back. "That's all the servants. The parents are out for the evening. But the son and daughter aren't accounted for!"

Suddenly Dade had pushed his way past the barriers.

"Hey, you!" shouted the chief. Two other fire fighters made a grab for him.

With an inhuman cry, Dade shook them off. He

leapt away. Then he was at the front door and was gone.

"Get him!" roared the chief. "That's all we need . . ."

A gust of flame shot up into the night as a section of the garage roof fell in. The molten outline of a car could be seen beneath it.

Someone in the crowd began to cheer.

"Pigs," shouted Jane. "Pigs!"

"Cook the rich," someone else shouted, and she heard whistles and catcalls.

Tears filled her eyes. How could people be so evil?

Then through the tears, she saw the front door open.

Around her, the jeers turned to cheers.

It was Dade. He had his arms around Cyndi. She was struggling with him, trying to pull free, trying to go back into the house.

"Let me go!" she cried. "Let me go!"

Another section of roof fell in.

Jane could feel the heat of the fire from all the way back where she stood.

Cyndi twisted as if she could feel the flames. "Dorian," she screamed. "Dorian!"

"Jane." In all the noise, she heard the soft voice.

"Char," she said gratefully, moving to let Char in beside her. "What are you doing here?"

Char put her hand on Jane's arm. "I was on my way home from the BurgerBurger. It's Dorian? He's in there?"

Jane nodded numbly. She saw Foy and Rick over Char's shoulder. Jane took a deep breath and said, "Georgina, too."

Rick said. "You're kidding. Georgina was in there, too?"

Shaking her head, Jane tried to explain. "No. But she's dead. They found her out on the Point tonight."

Char's face looked frozen, her eyes enormous. "Georgie? Like . . . like Wills?"

"Yes. At least, that's what it looked like. . . ."

Suddenly, the noise seemed to recede. It was just the four of them, staring at one another — Rick's face twitching, every emotion showing; Foy's unnaturally blank; Char's pale, paler; Jane's struggling for composure.

Then a fire fighter was escorting Dade and Cyndi toward them. Cyndi was crying.

No one had ever seen Cyndi cry before.

The fire fighter looked grim. "Stay here," he said. "I'll send a paramedic over."

"Dorian," wept Cyndi brokenly.

"Cyndi?" said Char.

"I killed him. I killed my own brother. The first time, I meant to, but I didn't. This time, I didn't mean it. *I didn't mean it.*"

In the cozy den in Jane's house, the fire burned softly, tamely in the grate. Cyndi held a mug of hot milk in her hands. The paramedic had given her something to calm her. She'd stopped crying.

Stopped talking. Now she just stared down at nothing.

They were waiting for her parents to be located and told the news.

"It's not your fault," said Jane again.

A long silence fell. Then Cyndi, not looking up, said tonelessly, "You don't know the whole story." Her fingers whitened on the mug. She raised it to her lips like a blind woman, held it there, her head bent.

Then she started to talk.

"Dorian and I hated each other," she said. "We used to do awful things to each other. It got so our parents had to hire different nannies, just to keep us separated.

"But we'd find ways to get together. And then we'd start on each other. Only we'd never admit what we were up to. It was always a game.

"Until one day, when Dorian and I were playing hide-and-seek. I was five. I hid in a cedar chest in the attic. Dorian found me. Only instead of letting me out, he locked the trunk.

"I don't know how long I was there. Hours. It was daylight when we started playing. It was dark when they found me.

"I thought I was going to die there.

"After that, I knew nothing would ever scare me again. And nothing was going to stop me from getting even with my brother."

"Cyndi," said Jane softly.

"Let me finish," said Cyndi harshly. "I waited.

Told Dorian I wanted to play hide-and-seek again. Pretended I really believed that the trunk had locked by accident.

"He hid in a closet. I think he thought he would jump out and really scare me.

"Only he didn't hear me. Not until I locked the door on him. Then I found some matches. I set fire to a wastebasket in the room.

"He smelled the smoke. He was terrified. He begged me to let him out. Just like I'd begged him. I wonder if he stayed and listened to me beg the way I stayed and listened to him. . . .

"We have a very good security system in our house. Always have. The fire department's connected directly to it. So they got there in time. I told them where he was. I was crying.

"I got into a lot of trouble for playing with matches.

"No one ever asked why Dorian was locked in the closet. But after that, we lived in separate wings of the house. Until we were older. Until we had 'outgrown' it.

"I was always bad after that," she said. "A bad girl."

A thin, ghastly smile crossed her face. "And Dorian was always very, very good."

"It's okay, Cyndi," said Dade.

Cyndi looked at him. "No. Because Dorian was in the garage tonight."

"Dorian?" repeated Jane.

"How do you know?" asked Dade.

"It's where he went when he left me. He was there with his car . . . his car . . ."

She took a deep shuddering breath.

"I think he'd been with Georgie. I think now, whatever was after Georgie, was after him.

"I think something is out there. And it's going to get us all."

Chapter 14

"That's crazy," said Rick.

Foy was shaking his head slowly.

Jane, meeting Charity's eyes, felt a tremor of fear go through her.

Char didn't think it was crazy.

Char believed Cyndi.

Dade looked past them all with a curious smile on his face.

Then a voice said, "She's right, more or less."

Jones walked into the room. For a moment, they were all silent. He didn't look any different. But something had changed. Something about him . . .

"How did you get in?" said Jane.

"The old-fashioned way," said Jones. He jerked his head toward the door. "Your guy let me in."

In spite of himself, Foy smiled, suddenly imagining how Hodges would react to being called "your guy."

Cyndi was regarding Jones with angry suspicion.

"You know what?" she said. "*Nothing* had ever happened until you got here. What have you got to say about that?"

Jones shrugged.

"No one was dead before you came along," Cyndi persisted, her voice low and threatening.

Jones shrugged again. "So? If I confess, will it make you feel better?"

Cyndi's head snapped up. "You're despicable."

Jones ignored her. His eyes met Char's. Looking at her, he said, "Something is out there. I'm not even sure what it is. But it is after us. Collectively. And individually."

Char took a shallow, sharp breath. Why was Jones looking at her?

"Great," said Rick. "It's big. It's bad. It's mad. And it's out there, looking for . . . us."

Char made an impatient gesture with her hand to silence Rick. "How do you know? Are you some kind of, some kind of supernatural bounty hunter?"

"How do we know it isn't some kind of trick," Foy drawled. "Maybe he's just some kind of a bounty hunter. Period."

"Three of us are dead," Jane pointed out.

"Us?" croaked Rick.

"This is stupid," said Cyndi. She was clenching and unclenching her hands. Whatever the doctor had given her wasn't working. "You're all stupid. Go away."

Jane put her hand on Cyndi's arm. Cyndi shuddered at the contact, and huddled down again.

"Someone killed Wills on Halloween night. Three days later, in the same place, Georgie is dead. And Dorian — "

"Is burned alive." Dade finished Jones's sentence.

"What happened to Dorian could have been an accident. It's not the same as what happened to Wills and to Georgie," said Foy.

Cyndi started to rock slowly in her chair. Her voice, when she spoke, was almost a singsong. "It wasn't an accident. I saw it."

"You saw it *happen*?" Jones's voice sharpened.

"I saw it on the door. Dorian's car. He came back tonight, and I was waiting when he pulled into the garage. Scared. Scared. Scared."

"Cyndi," said Jane softly.

"So scared. I thought it was a joke. I thought Rick did it."

"Hey!" said Rick. "I haven't done anything!"

Jane gave Cyndi a quick shake. "Cyndi! What are you talking about?"

For a moment, Cyndi didn't move. Then she seemed suddenly transformed. Her lips curled back in a sneer. "What am I talking about? Tonight, when Dorian got home, I saw his car in the garage. Something had made gouges all down the side of the car. And on the handle of the driver's door, there was a hook."

Everyone stared at Cyndi, at the gleeful, awful smile on her face. "A hook," she said. "A hook. Just like that stupid story of Rick's."

And, then, just as suddenly, Cyndi retreated back into herself, seemed to shrink and grow smaller, pulling her legs up and wrapping her arms around them, pressing her forehead to her knees. "Go away," she moaned.

"*I* didn't do it," said Rick.

"That book," said Char. "The one *you* gave me, Jones." She didn't wait for him to confirm or deny her statement. "It talks about something that happened in Point Harbor when it was a whaling port. Something that caused ships to sink, that haunted — is that the right word, Jones — that haunted Cemetery Point. Not just out there, but the whole town."

Rick said, "What book?"

"Shh," ordered Dade.

Jones nodded.

"And it got stopped. Somehow."

She waited. Jones said, slowly, almost as if he were in pain, "I don't know how."

This time, he didn't quite meet Char's eyes. She said, softly, "Don't you?"

Foy said slowly, "Something inhuman. That got . . . dead and buried, would you say? Out there, in the graveyard? For a long, long time?"

"Dead and buried," agreed Jones.

"Until something woke it up," said Foy.

Although she was sitting with her back close to the fire, Char felt the chill on her neck.

"We woke it up, didn't we, Jones? That night.

Halloween night," said Char. "We went to a party in a graveyard and we woke the dead."

The fire had started to die out. Cyndi's parents had come and gone. Cyndi was staying with Jane that night.

Horror makes strange bedfellows, thought Char wryly.

The cops had been there, too. Dorian had been in the garage. They'd found his body. They were looking at a possible link between Georgie's death and Dorian's, the cops said. Murder–suicide, they said.

No one bothered to disagree.

They sat still by the dying fire, listening as Char finished reading aloud from the book.

"So it *has* been around for a long, long time," said Jane. "They *must* have buried whatever it was — is — out there on Cemetery Point, maybe did something to make it stay put, like how they bury vampires with a stake through the heart. . . ."

"And closed up the joint," said Dade.

"Until we came along," said Jane.

Cyndi, who had resumed her motionless pose in her chair, with her forehead resting on her drawn-up knees, sing-songed, "It's my party and I'll cry if I want to, die if I want to . . ."

"We can't trust *anyone*," said Jones. "Not the cops. Not our parents. Not our friends."

"Look around," said Dade genially. "We're all friends here."

Rick broke in. "We should tell the cops."

"Right," said Foy. "Like we're going to tell the cops: 'Oh, Officer, there's a serial killer out there. It likes knives and fire. And it isn't human and has superhuman powers.' "

"Supernatural powers," whispered Jane.

"We can't trust anyone," insisted Jones. "Think about what we just heard. Think! Whatever it is, it has supernatural powers."

"It can change shapes," said Char abruptly. "That's what that meant: 'Power to mimic form and life and shadow.' "

"No way," said Rick. "Get real."

Foy interceded. "We have to do a little reality check here. Something — or someone — is stalking us. Maybe it's some flipped-wig weirdo we unwrapped when we did the graveyard party. *Maybe.* But an old book and a bunch of words are *not* what's real in all this."

"I hope it turns into a babe, a built blonde babe, before it goes after me," said Rick.

"God, Rick, you're disgusting." Cyndi roused herself to give Rick a withering look.

"Why don't you believe me?" asked Char.

"I don't know what to believe," whispered Jane.

"So what're we supposed to do while this alleged supernatural serial chopper is in town?" snarled Cyndi. "Only travel in threes for the rest of our lives?"

"I don't even think threes would do it," answered Jones.

No one had a comeback for that.

The silence fell again. Char listened to the sound of the wind outside. Cold, cold wind. Cold as death.

Cold as the thing that stalked them. Char believed in it now. Whatever it was, it had no human feelings. If it had ever been alive, it was no more. It would not understand mercy, or pity. Or love.

It wouldn't matter to it that Wills, crazy, mean Wills, might have been something different someday. Something better. Something good.

It wouldn't care about Georgie's energy and dreams, and why she'd had them, and what had made them so much too big for her. Dreams that Georgie would never make real-life sized, now.

It wouldn't care that Dorian was dead, horribly, in the way he feared the most. Gone forever.

It wasn't human. Or even alive.

But it was real. A hunger. An evil inhuman force.

So much bigger and stronger than any of them could ever be.

It didn't even matter if they hated it, feared it. It didn't do any good. It didn't matter at all.

Rick, for once not joking, said, "We're all going to die. Is that what you're saying Jones?"

"God," said Foy softly.

"No!" shrieked Cyndi. "I'm not. You can't make me. I'm going to fight! I'll stop it. I'll . . ."

She jumped up. Dade grabbed her shoulders. "Cyndi!"

"No!" she screamed and, with almost superhuman strength, tore loose from Dade and ran out of the room.

"Stop her," commanded Jones. "We have to stop her!"

Chapter 15

Cyndi ran wildly down the long driveway toward the shadow of the hedges. The front door swung wide behind her.

It was almost uncanny, how fast she could run.

They ran after her, into the night.

But Cyndi was faster. Char heard a car door open. Then a car shrieked out of the shadows, bearing down on them, accelerating.

Char had one glimpse of Cyndi's white, mad face, and then she threw herself out of the way.

The car swept by without even stopping.

Rolling to her feet, she caught Jones's arm. "Your car!" she cried. "Cyndi took your car."

"Let's go," said Dade, wheeling without breaking stride. "In mine."

It was like the Keystone Cops, thought Char dazedly. The way they piled into Dade's car. How many potential murder victims can you get in a heavy metal Chevy?

The needle on the car shot upward from zero to

seventy in no time. Dade cornered on two wheels, sat the car back down, and hammered it into the dark.

"We'll catch her," he said. "This car can do it."

Then he glanced sideways quickly at Jones. "But, then, maybe yours can, too."

Jones didn't say anything. He just jerked his head forward in a nod, once.

The taillights of the disappearing car were a bloody smear in the darkness.

Why didn't the cops appear out of nowhere, like they usually did? wondered Char. Why weren't they lurking, waiting to yank some kid's chain?

As if he could read her thoughts, Dade said, "I hate the cops."

"They're probably all out at the Point," said Foy.

"It's been hours," Char said. "Maybe they've sealed it off and all gone home."

"Well, they're not around here," said Rick.

It was true. No cops. Nobody at all. No one was on the road except them. And Cyndi.

"It's like the lights are on, but no one is home — anywhere," muttered Char. Beside her, she felt Jane's hand on her arm.

The distance between the cars stopped widening. But it didn't grow any narrower.

They were traveling at the speed of light.

No. At the speed of darkness.

Then Jane gave a little gasp. "The Back Bay. She's going down the Back Bay Road."

Char said, "To the Point."

"Let's hope the cops *are* still there," said Dade grimly.

Jones said, so softly that only Char heard, "They won't be."

"We're not going back out there?" croaked Rick incredulously.

"We don't have a choice," Foy shot back.

"*I* have a choice," snapped Rick. "I'm not going out there."

Without slowing down, Dade said, "You wanna get out, be my guest. The door's right there."

For a moment, Char thought Rick might actually do it. Then he said sullenly, "Dade, you're jack crazy, you know that? Like I'm gonna hit the blacktop doing ninety."

"Then you're in for the haul," said Dade.

He pushed the accelerator.

The wheels didn't even touch the ground on that curve, thought Char dispassionately. Beside her, Jane's hand tightened on her arm, then relaxed.

Jane the calm, thought Char. Or maybe she's just gone fatal. Then she caught a glimpse of Jane's pale, set face. And saw the direction of her gaze.

Jane wasn't staring out at the night, screaming by the window. She wasn't staring at the red lights ahead that had just turned down the road to Cemetery Point.

She was staring at Dade.

True love, thought Char. Spare me.

"She's got to stop for the gate, man," said Rick.

"Don't count on it," said Dade.

"Look out!" screamed Rick.

Dade didn't even slow down.

"Did you hit it?" asked Rick.

"I don't know," said Dade tersely.

Jane said firmly, "He didn't hit it, whatever it was."

Rick gave a half-hysterical laugh. "Yeah. Good. That's what's important here."

"Maybe it wasn't anything at all," said Jones softly.

And Char felt the hair on her neck rise again. *Shape-changer*, she thought.

Able to skitter out on a road and make a car go over a cliff?

"Jones," she said softly.

"Yes," he said. And she knew he was answering her unspoken question.

Even if she didn't know how he knew.

They'd slowed down a little now. The road was just as bumpy as it had been on Halloween night. The trees leaned in just as closely. Only the moon wasn't full.

Char was afraid. But this time, it wasn't a pleasurable fear. It wasn't the comfortable creepy-crawlies of Halloween, the little thrill at the idea that a witch or a ghost might be lurking just out of sight, just out of belief, dressed up in childhood story-clothes, something familiar and simple. Your basic Halloween apparition.

This was real.

This was death.

"Look out!" Foy, this time, leaning forward to peer over Dade's shoulder.

Dade slowed fractionally.

The metal gate was burst apart, twisted all out of recognition.

"Your car's dead, fella," said Dade to Jones.

But it wasn't. Somewhere just ahead, the red of the taillights kept flickering in and out as Jones's car disappeared down the trail.

"It should be dead," said Char. "What's that car made of, Jones?"

"Kryptonite," said Jones.

"I wish," said Dade. He fought the wheel, scraping trees, bucking the car over ruts and through the sand.

And then they were in the clearing.

Dade slammed on the brakes. The Chevy slewed sideways. Kicked back as he wrestled with the wheel.

Then it shuddered to a stop.

Inches away from Jones's car.

The front of Jones's car was twisted all out of recognition, the glass broken, one light on, the other shattered and dead. The driver's door was open.

Cyndi was nowhere in sight.

"We're heeere," Rick said feebly.

No one even bothered to tell him what to do with it.

Char took a long, shaky breath. "What are we going to do?"

"Let's go," said Foy.

Jane glanced at Foy in surprise. Foy wasn't usually a leader. Not a follower. But not a leader, either.

Char said, "No, wait." Staring out at the dark, she asked, "Have you thought of this? Maybe that's not Cyndi up there, leading us all out here. Maybe it's not Cyndi at all."

Chapter 16

"Not," said Rick.

"We were with her all night," said Jane.

"We weren't with her when her brother died," said Char softly.

A shaken, disbelieving silence answered her.

Then Jones said calmly, "Whatever. We need to stay together. That's critical."

Jane said, "We could hold hands. Form a chain."

"Or, how 'bout the buddy system." Rick tried for sarcasm.

"Holding hands is not a bad idea," said Jones. He got out of the car and held out his hand to Char.

"Let's do it." Taking a flashlight out from under the seat, Dade jumped out, pulling Jane with him with his free hand.

Foy took Jane's hand.

"I want you to know, Foy, that this doesn't mean we're going steady," said Rick. Unexpectedly, Dade gave a crack of laughter.

This is how it started, Char thought. We were

all holding hands in a circle around the fire. Taking Rick's other hand, she suddenly remembered something. "Lara," she said. "What about Lara?"

"She's still at home," said Jane.

"At least *she's* safe," put in Rick.

With Dade leading and Jones bringing up the rear, they walked across the clearing. One by one they stepped out of the light and into the darkness, clumsy, stumbling, following the pale beam of the flashlight into the woods.

"Anybody know the words to 'Chain of Fools,' " quipped Rick.

Foy groaned, and Jane gave a nervous giggle.

Rick began to sing. Foy groaned again and said, "Don't sing."

"Think of it as a secret weapon," said Rick. He kept on singing.

"It's ruining the element of surprise," suggested Foy.

"I dunno," said Dade. "I'm surprised. At how bad he sings."

"What are you thinking about?" Jones asked softly. He was walking just at Char's shoulder. She felt his breath on her ear.

Turning her head slightly toward him, she whispered back, "Sunrise. I was thinking how in the vampire movies, the sun always comes up."

"Usually following a period of extreme darkness," said Jones.

"In the movies, it's when the vampire dies."

Rick began the chorus of "I Heard It Through the Grapevine."

Typical Rick, Char thought. But the sound did push back the dark. A little. She could still feel the silence, the waiting stillness just beyond.

"What are you thinking?" she asked Jones quickly, willing the silence away.

"You can't see anything if you look at it head-on in the dark. It works better if you look a little to one side."

"We have a tree in our backyard," said Char randomly. "I used to like to sit in it at night and look into our house. You could see everyone, like in a play. I never used to believe they couldn't see me. I thought they were just pretending."

"The light makes the dark pretty intense," said Jones. "It's all in how you look at it, I guess."

"Blinded by the light," said Char. "Not very useful."

"Unless it helps to see what you're afraid of."

"Unless it scares you to death. . . ."

"If you let something scare you to death, then the worst has happened," said Jones.

"This is comforting," said Char. "Should my life be in danger, remind me."

"I will." Jones squeezed her hand.

The silence fell again.

Ahead, Dade said, "We're here." The beam of the flashlight bored through the trees.

They'd reached the graveyard.

Rick stopped singing abruptly. Char felt how cold Rick's hand was in hers. And how warm Jones's was.

Dade took his breath in sharply.

"Uh-oh," said Rick. For once, he didn't sound like he was trying to be funny.

Something was waiting for them up ahead.

Dade kept walking. Behind him, the human chain stretched out to breaking point.

Dade raised the flashlight.

"I love parties," said Cyndi. "It's time for a party. Don't you love parties?"

"It's time for this one to be over," said Dade.

Cyndi smiled. "I love parties," she repeated.

Keeping his flashlight on Cyndi, Dade stopped. "Hey, Cyndi? This has been done. It's old. Let's go somewhere else."

"Okay," said Cyndi, still smiling. "Let's." She leaned forward — then snatched the flashlight and threw it up in the air. As it fell, she turned and darted into the dark.

Dade dropped Jane's hand. "Cyndi," he shouted and plunged after her.

Jane hesitated only a moment. Then she wrenched her hand out of Foy's and started after Dade.

Behind Char, Jones raised his voice desperately. "Stay together! We have to stay together!"

But it was too late.

"This is bad," said Rick harshly. "This is crazy. We've got to get out of here. We can't . . ."

"Settle down, Rick," said Foy.

In answer, Rick pulled his hand free of Char's and yanked so hard on Foy's hand that Foy almost fell. But he regained his balance and the two of them began to circle in a grotesque dance, pulling on each other.

"Calm down," Foy said.

"Let go, man, let go!"

"C'mon," pleaded Foy. "If we're not going steady, I don't want to dance. . . ."

"Let go!" shrieked Rick.

Without warning, Foy raised his arm. He punched Rick in the jaw. Rick's head snapped back. He staggered. Then he fell like a stone.

Letting go of Rick's hand, Foy bent over him. "Out cold," he announced.

"I don't believe you did that," said Char.

"Now he can't run away," said Foy, rubbing his knuckles.

"And he can't stay with us, now, either," said Jones. "Unless we carry him."

"Why?" asked Foy impatiently.

"We can't leave him here. Not by himself."

"Listen," said Foy. "What did you want me to do? Let him tear out of here like everyone else?"

Char stopped listening. She was frowning. It wasn't the silence that was bothering her. What was it?

And then she realized what it was. The darkness. It was gone. The moon was out, flickering in and out among the clouds that blew above.

But there was no wind.

In the unnatural moon-strobe, she watched Foy and Jones. Jones had let go of her hand. He and Foy were propping Rick up against the wall, trying to get him to wake up.

Just like on television, she thought dreamily. Just like when I used to sit in that tree . . .

A vast lethargy washed over her. She wanted to sit down next to Rick. To go to sleep.

She yawned hugely.

"I'm getting the flashlight," she said.

She giggled. How mortifying, she thought. I never giggle.

Rick groaned.

Something moved in the corner of her eye.

No. No, it was the flashlight.

"Char," said Jones.

"I'll be right there," she said. "I'm just going to get that flashlight. . . ."

"Wait."

"No no no . . . now don't worry. I'll be right over. . . ." Like a sleepwalker, she turned in the direction of the flashlight.

Rick let out a yell and came to, swinging and punching.

Leaving them to scuffle, she strolled into the dark.

There. There it was.

She bent to pick it up. And saw the writing on the tombstone.

Chapter 17

"No," she whispered.

"Char!" Jones's voice.

She ignored him. Picking up the flashlight, she turned it on the gravemarker.

CHARITY WEBSTER
1888–

At least I'm not dead yet, she thought, and felt the bubble of hysterical laughter rise in her throat.

"Char." Jones was closer now.

Jones.

Jones knew . . .

Knew what?

Then he was beside her. She'd begun to shake. The light shimmied in her hand. But she held on to it, even when Jones tried to pry her fingers loose.

"No," she said.

Then she turned the light on him.

The light made his face look bleached and old.

He held up his hand to shield his eyes, wincing. "You're blinding me," he said.

"Not me," she said. "The light."

"Char," he said.

"No. No, you tell me. Tell me *now*. What is going on here?"

"If I knew . . ."

"You knew about that book. *You're* the one who gave it to me. Where did you get it?"

"I can't explain now."

"When I'm dead is *too* late. Way too late."

"You're hysterical."

"Why do guys always say that?" She laughed. Good. That stupid giggle was gone.

She was trembling. She was afraid. No. No, she felt powerful. Strong.

Immortal.

She felt the power rising up through her body. More scalding than any passion. More dangerous than love . . .

A terrible shudder rocked the earth.

She stumbled. Watched indifferently as the flashlight fell from her hand and went out.

Again the earth moved. There was a roaring sound this time. A rending sound.

Was it a loud sound? She couldn't tell. Sensations poured over her, a thousand impressions, each distinct and clear. Her human senses were gone. This was something more. Something much, much more.

In the darkness, she saw Jones's mouth move.

But she couldn't hear him.

She smelled it first. A familiar smell, somehow. Rank and ashy.

She heard it next. The light tread of something heavy. Something heavy and extremely quick. Something hunting.

Then she felt it.

It was standing behind her.

She closed her eyes, and the terrible power coursing through her brought with it a vision.

A woman was standing at the edge of the sea. The water boiled around her. The smoke of torches lingered in the air. But the others were gone. They'd run away.

They'd left her there.

Not me, thought Char. The woman is *not* me.

She opened her eyes. She was still in the cemetery. And it was still behind her.

But a grave's length away, another figure waited, pale and shimmering by the graveyard wall.

It was the woman. The woman from her vision. The woman from her dreams.

"Who are you?" Char whispered. "What do you want?"

The woman raised her arms.

Char took a step forward.

It was as if she'd been punched in the chest. Gasping, she stopped. Roaring filled her ears. But beneath the roar, a fierce and ancient voice whispered, "Turn. Turn. Turn."

Char turned.

A river of fire poured toward her.

Run, something inside her screamed.

She crouched for flight. "Stay," commanded the woman's voice. And with the voice came that sense of scalding, dangerous power.

Char obeyed the voice.

The woman owned her now. Char had been chosen. And she had made her choice.

The molten river parted and sank into the earth around her with a hiss.

Trembling with mortal fear and immortal rage, Char faced the thing that now waited in the shadows before her.

A black cloud covered the moon. The darkness was complete.

The shadows began to move, writhing, with an eerie shrill sound and the sucking of the air. Unmoving, she watched.

Without breathing. Without thinking.

A figure walked out of the contorted dark.

"What do you want?" it mocked. If the woman's voice was a fierce and ancient whisper, this voice was shudderingly smooth, warmly seductive.

"Lara?" Char asked.

"That's right," Lara said. "It's me."

"No," said Char. "You're not Lara. Lara's safe."

"No one's safe from *me*." The figure pirouetted, then dipped in a curtsy. "I took Wills. And then I took Lara. Do you believe me?"

Jones said, "No, you didn't . . ."

"Silence!" Lara lashed the air with her arm, and Char heard Jones gasp and stumble and then thud against the gravestone. Her gravestone.

"Jones?" she said. For a fraction of a second, she became herself. She turned her head.

"No!" said the woman's voice, and Char looked back at the thing that had taken Lara's shape.

"Ah!" Lara stopped. But she was much closer now. The bloody princess dress she wore moved of its own accord, tugged by invisible eddies, unspeakable tides.

"Is this a game?" asked Char. "Like blindman's bluff?"

"No game," purred Lara.

Char stepped back.

"Ah," said the woman's voice, much closer now.

Lara smiled. She took two steps forward. "I've been waiting for you," she said.

"You're not Lara!"

"But I could be. . . ." It tilted its head coquettishly. "If you were Lara and you met me, would that scare you?"

"NO!"

"Oh, dear," said Lara mockingly. She smiled, and the smile began to split her face.

Char took another step back and another.

And felt something brush her shoulder.

"It's me," said the woman's voice. Char waited for her to continue, to say, "Don't be afraid."

But the woman didn't.

Instead, her hand closed on Char's shoulder. Where it touched her was cold. But the power in her surged up to meet it, making her back arch as

155

if she were caught in an electric current. "Now," said the woman. But the voice was no longer a whisper in Char's ear. It was in her, in her mouth. How can I feel so helpless? thought Char. How . . .

Char felt her lips move. She heard her voice say, "It's me."

Her voice. The woman's words.

The thing wearing Lara's face smiled. And now another face began to pulse into shape beneath the rims of flesh.

"Yess . . ." said the lips, and the thing took two steps forward.

The rotting, scorching smell filled Char's lungs.

She couldn't breathe.

She was going to die.

"No," she gasped.

She rocked back. She would run. Save herself.

But she couldn't

I won't give up, thought Char. I won't, I . . .

She lunged forward and seized the Ripper in her arms.

And it was Wills she held, Wills dead, Wills dying.

"Help me," he pleaded. "Help meee. . . ."

"I can't," she said. He was so strong. But she held on. She didn't look away.

The figure threw back its demon head and howled. There was a sound of skin splitting like ripe fruit. Beneath the shining blood now, the face of Georgina looked back at Char.

"You hated me," she hissed. "You killed me."

"I was wrong," Char gasped. "But I didn't kill you."

It twisted wildly in her arms. The shedding layer of skin felt like an old blouse over her arms. The thing raised its head and locked eyes with her.

"You could save us now," said Dorian's voice. "Let me go."

"No," she said.

"Let me GO!"

"NO!" she said between gritted teeth.

Dorian's face tore open before her eyes.

And she saw herself.

"Mirror, mirror, on the wall," it said. Her face. Her voice.

Her smile.

"What you see is what you get," it said. And Char felt her own body. Felt it turn to slime and gore beneath her hands. Saw her own lips draw back and spit: blood and gobbets of flesh.

She held on.

The pain began. The awful grief. For the killing. For the rage. For the eternity of loneliness.

Her own pain. Her own grief.

And the woman's

She tightened her hold.

Something sharp as death pierced her above the heart.

Her heart contracted with sorrow and pain.

And awful joy.

Then the thing gave one last shape-rending twist in her mortal arms and the earth tore open beneath her feet and she was falling and as she fell she knew she was falling into her own grave where it had waited for so long.

No. Not her grave.

I am not you, Char told the woman who possessed her. And at that moment, with a pain more awful than any imagining, Char felt the power that had taken her begin to subside. The phantom woman, her other self, had been received into the earth. Char was alone inside herself now. She was free.

Behind her, as Char fell into the grave, the sun began to rise. And the thing in her arms began to howl.

Rest in peace, thought Char, and the howl began to dwindle and die as the earth closed over them all.

And she held on.

Chapter 18

She was in a grave. Buried alive. It had her by the ankle. Pulling her deeper as the earth shuddered and sealed itself together over her face.

She kicked. Tried to breathe and tasted dirt and whatever graves were made of. Gagged.

And then she was blinded by the light.

It was morning.

She sat up. She was safe. It was over. She was in her own bedroom. In a little while, it would be time to get up. She had the whole day ahead of her.

She had the rest of her life.

Jones pulled his car into the overlook. Char got out and walked to the rail and looked out at the Point. It was just a curve of land in the water now. Not so big a curve as it used to be. The morning after she'd met the Ripper, a chunk of the Point had torn away and fallen into the ocean. The grave-yard was gone.

But that had been a while ago. Autumn was turning into winter now. The nightmares were going away. The killings had ended.

"Hey," said Jones.

Char turned to him and smiled. "Hey."

"You did good," said Jones.

"I didn't have a choice, did I?"

"I'm sorry," he said.

"It's okay." She shrugged. "You made up for it when you grabbed my ankle and hauled me up out of that grave."

"You saved us all. It was the least I could do."

She suddenly grinned. "Just admit it, Jones. You couldn't keep your hands off me."

High above, an arrowhead of geese started their descent for a landing. Their honking sounded clear and strong on the cold air.

Char said thoughtfully, "It was her. She needed me to help her be buried *inside* the graveyard. That was her grave on the outside. She'd stopped it somehow, and they thought she'd made an unholy pact with it. That's why they kept her out.

"And whoever kept that journal had a grave made for her inside, just in case.

"She had my name. . . ."

"Whoever she was," said Jones, "she took the Ripper with her."

"We raised that thing, didn't we, that night at Cyndi's party?" She didn't wait for Jones to answer, but went on. "If we hadn't done that, Wills, Georgie, Dorian — they might all still be alive."

"But if we hadn't done it, something else might

have wakened it up. And because you did, that first Charity had a chance to rest in peace at last."

"I hope she is," said Charity. She paused. "But is the Ripper dead?"

"The graveyard is gone," said Jones. "I don't know. Maybe it just changed shape again."

"I thought it had gotten Lara, too," Char said. "That's what the Ripper told me. You tried to warn me that it was a trick."

"Just another gruesome trick . . . to confuse you. To distract you," said Jones. "I don't think Lara saw the Ripper. I think she just saw enough to scare her out of her wits." He paused.

"But it would have gotten Lara, too. It would have gotten all of us. Each killing made it stronger."

Char asked, for about the hundredth time, "How did you know what would happen?"

And for about the hundredth time, Jones answered, "I didn't."

"What about the book?"

"I found it in my travels," Jones said. "I believe everything I read."

"But why me? Why my name? When I saw it on that tombstone . . ."

Jones said, "You can't believe everything you read." He pulled her closer to him.

She didn't have time to ask him the other question: Who are you?

The last time she'd asked, he hadn't answered, as usual. Instead, he'd said, "Have you ever thought about who you are? I mean, if you were named another name, would you still be you? Take away your name, and what you do, and where you live, and who your parents are. Then tell me who you really are."

Once, the idea would have bothered her. Now, it made a sort of sense. So she left the question for the others.

Like the questions about where he came from, and where he was going. Those were answers nobody had. Not for their own life. Not for anyone else's.

"Hey! Hey!" Dade's voice. He'd pulled up to the edge of the overlook and was leaning out the window. Jane was with him. She leaned across Dade and said, "Char. Come on. We're going over to Lara's."

"Who's we?" asked Jones.

"You know — Foy, Rick, Cyndi." Jane made an airy motion with her hand. "Like that."

"The usual party animals," said Dade, grinning.

"Later," said Char.

"Serious," said Dade. He kicked his car into gear and took off.

"Sorry," said Char. "I should've asked. Did you want to go?"

"Later," said Jones. He leaned closer. "But for now, I like this party here just fine."

point® THRILLERS

R.L. Stine
- ☐ MC44236-8 The Baby-sitter — $3.25
- ☐ MC44332-1 The Baby-sitter II — $3.25
- ☐ MC45386-6 Beach House — $3.25
- ☐ MC43278-8 Beach Party — $3.25
- ☐ MC43125-0 Blind Date — $3.25
- ☐ MC43279-6 The Boyfriend — $3.25
- ☐ MC44333-X The Girlfriend — $3.25
- ☐ MC45385-8 Hit and Run — $3.25
- ☐ MC43280-X The Snowman — $3.25
- ☐ MC43139-0 Twisted — $3.25

Caroline B. Cooney
- ☐ MC44316-X The Cheerleader — $3.25
- ☐ MC41641-3 The Fire — $3.25
- ☐ MC43806-9 The Fog — $3.25
- ☐ MC45681-4 Freeze Tag (11/92) — $3.25
- ☐ MC45402-1 The Perfume — $3.25
- ☐ MC44884-6 Return of the Vampire — $2.95
- ☐ MC41640-5 The Snow — $3.25

Diane Hoh
- ☐ MC44330-5 The Accident — $3.25
- ☐ MC45401-3 The Fever — $3.25
- ☐ MC43050-5 Funhouse — $3.25
- ☐ MC44904-4 The Invitation — $2.95
- ☐ MC45640-7 The Train (9/92) — $3.25

Sinclair Smith
- ☐ MC45063-8 The Waitress — $2.95

Christopher Pike
- ☐ MC43014-9 Slumber Party — $3.25
- ☐ MC44256-2 Weekend — $3.25

A. Bates
- ☐ MC45829-9 The Dead Game (12/92) — $3.25
- ☐ MC43291-5 Final Exam — $3.25
- ☐ MC44582-0 Mother's Helper — $2.95
- ☐ MC44238-4 Party Line — $3.25

B.E. Atkins
- ☐ MC45246-0 Mirror, Mirror — $3.25
- ☐ MC45349-1 The Ripper (10/92) — $3.25
- ☐ MC44941-9 Sister Dearest — $2.95

Carol Ellis
- ☐ MC44768-8 My Secret Admirer — $3.25
- ☐ MC44916-8 The Window — $2.95

Richie Tankersley Cusick
- ☐ MC43115-3 April Fools — $3.25
- ☐ MC43203-6 The Lifeguard — $3.25
- ☐ MC43114-5 Teacher's Pet — $3.25
- ☐ MC44235-X Trick or Treat — $3.25

Lael Littke
- ☐ MC44237-6 Prom Dress — $3.25

Edited by T. Pines
- ☐ MC45256-8 Thirteen — $3.50

Available wherever you buy books, or use this order form.

Scholastic Inc., P.O. Box 7502, 2931 East McCarty Street, Jefferson City, MO 65102

Please send me the books I have checked above. I am enclosing $_____ (please add $2.00 to cover shipping and handling). Send check or money order — no cash or C.O.D.s please.

Name _____

Address _____

City _____ State/Zip _____

Please allow four to six weeks for delivery. Offer good in the U.S. only. Sorry, mail orders are not available to residents of Canada. Prices subject to change.

PT192

point

Other books you will enjoy, about real kids like you!